OF DREAMS AND KINGS AND MYSTICAL THINGS

A Novel of the Life of King David

Joyce Strong

Destiny Image Fiction

An Imprint of
Destiny Image® Publishers, Inc.
P.O. Box 310
Shippensburg, PA 17257-0310

"For where your treasure is,
there will your heart be also." Matthew 6:21

ISBN 0-7684-3044-5

For Worldwide Distribution
Printed in the U.S.A.

This book and all other Destiny Image, Revival Press, MercyPlace, Fresh Bread, Destiny Image Fiction, and Treasure House books are available at Christian bookstores and distributors worldwide.

For a U.S. bookstore nearest you, call **1-800-722-6774**.
For more information on foreign distributors, call **717-532-3040**.
Or reach us on the Internet:
www.destinyimage.com

THE FLOW OF DAVID'S LIFE

PREFACE

While King David's devotion to God and his understanding of God's ways inspire us and increase our hunger for intimacy with God, that same devotion and understanding also give rise to many questions.

What caused David to anticipate with such joy the coming of the King of kings, even though he would not live to see Him on earth face to face? How could he have so thoroughly comprehended God's sovereignty and faithfulness as to have trusted Him totally? Where had he learned such love and awe for the Father that at a word he would fall on his face in repentance? What did he understand of Heaven that caused him to so easily forgive as he had been forgiven? What gave him such a keen sense of redemption?

David's grasp of eternal things surely necessitated encounters with the living God. The shape and fabric of those encounters have been left for us to imagine.

Of Dreams and Kings and Mystical Things weaves a story of what might well have been. This book does not seek to rewrite the Bible in order to form its own conclusions, but rather uses the clues tucked away within the character, the writings, and the times of David and his contemporaries to help us today understand spiritual truths and become intimate with the God who loves us.

As we track David's spiritual journey from his youth to the end of his life on earth, the same questions that gripped his heart will test ours. Through it all, we too will look into the eyes of the Lamb and know the heart of the King.

5

HOW TO USE THIS BOOK

This book can be used in leadership training classes to generate discussion on the timeless issues of leadership that David faced and over which he often agonized, issues that are subtly woven into the fabric of the story of this great king.

Of Dreams and Kings and Mystical Things is a book that you will use over and over and want to share with others who, like you, desire to understand and have the heart of the King of kings.

(All Scriptures are taken from the New International Version of the Bible.)

Part I

EYES OF THE LAMB

Chapter One

VISION IN THE NIGHT SKY

The pungent aroma of the evening sacrifice pierced David's reverie. The melody that his mind had been chasing all day still stirred restlessly about him in the air, teasing him to capture it and give it sound and cadence. But it would have to wait. His father was calling him to come in from the field.

After carefully nestling his lyre among the folds of his bedroll, the lean and sun-browned 12-year-old turned toward his father's voice, and then set out at a run to join his family on the hillside a short distance away.

The altar stood on the crest of the hill in sharp relief against the setting sun. His heart jumped at the sight of it, his emotions strangely and deeply moved. The scene held the same power for him time after time! He vaguely wondered if his brothers ever felt what he did....

"Has chasing dumb sheep made you hard of hearing, David?" his brother Abinadab chided him good-naturedly. Then seriously, Abinadab added, "Father had to call you three times before you heard him!"

Eliab was not so kind. "I wish I could lounge around all day with nothing to do but watch lazy sheep, fend off puny coyotes, and sing senseless songs to the wind!"

Spitting disdainfully into the sand and then cocking his head, Eliab sent a mocking look straight into David's eyes as he added, "Well, what does it matter? You're not going to amount to a thing anyway, kid."

David mustered a wry smile in order to fend off the derision in his brother's words. Why Eliab had to be so mean to him was something that David couldn't understand.

Heaving a deep sigh, the shepherd boy turned again toward the setting sun and the sacrifice that crowned the small hill at the edge of the tiny village. The sweet aroma once again overpowered his senses.

His stomach felt queasy as his eyes sought the remains of the lamb upon the stone altar. He had held it in his arms many times. Memories of only a year ago flooded his mind as he thought back to the first day of its life. When the tiny lamb had taken tumble after tumble in the soft, cool grass of that early morning, David had laughed with delight. How quickly in the following days it had learned to walk steadily on those four new legs!

As David's ears caught the soft crackle of the altar's fire, he recalled the lamb's soft, dark eyes. *Could the lamb have known how its life would end?* he wondered.

David absently pushed sand around with one foot as he stood there, lost in the memories of the lamb.

As the reality of the present moment overtook him, tears welled up in the young shepherd's eyes. He brushed them away before Eliab could see them and ridicule him again.

The Vision

A sudden flash of movement in the heavens startled him. Instantly his eyes turned to the sky.

The lad caught his breath as the strangest figures began to form high above him while the orange sunset eased into shades of rose and purple.

There to the north...what was that? Winged dragons! Could it be? He rubbed his eyes to clear them, but the dragons were still there!

Breathing fire and looking hatefully toward earth, they shot this way and that, as though intent upon burning holes in the velvet sky. Their talons were monstrously long, and their wings stirred the night air into gales!

Then out of the south, as great and brilliant as the dragons were horrid, arose a host of angels brandishing swords in their right hands!

Lightning played about the powerful, glistening creatures as they prepared to charge the malevolent dragons that swirled in the storm above them.

Just as they were about to engage in battle, the blast of a trumpet split the sky, sounding from somewhere beyond the stars in the distance. It ripped through the air, strangely fusing all the heavens into one glorious mural of victory somehow yet to come.

Who blew the trumpet, David could not tell. But he hardly had time to wonder before the scene changed before him.

From the east and from the west, pressing in upon his vision from opposite directions, moved two enormous shards of wood! Rough-hewn beams—one vertical and one horizontal—forged their way across the sky as if carried by some invisible giants. As they met, they shifted into place upon one another, forming a great "T" in the heavens.

The trumpet's call continued as a figure—not unlike that of one of the shepherds with whom he kept company—strode with purpose toward the crossed beams.

But as the simple, sandaled figure neared the beams, his image was transformed! In his place there stood a King—a regal King dressed in a flowing, white linen robe gathered at the waist by a golden sash. On His head rested a crown of pure gold, studded with jewels of every color.

The King's face was weathered by warfare, yet soft with compassion; His bearing majestic, yet gentle and inviting.

As the King looked down at David, His loving eyes pierced David's heart to the core! In awe and with no debate, David then and there pledged his allegiance forever to this

13

King who had set his heart ablaze in the space of a single moment.

The Conflict

Then, as if by some strange compulsion, the King backed up against the crossed beams, spreading His arms to conform to the wood's design. As He pressed against the beams, He found Himself held fast to their rough surface.

And then it seemed to David that evil of every kind, like great leaden spears, flew at the captive monarch, piercing Him again and again!

As the very air surrounding the King shriveled up with the pain, His death began. The great love and agony that gripped the heavens, gripped David's soul as well as he gazed upon the scene, appalled.

As this regal monarch hung upon the rugged beams, His eyes took on the very look David had so often seen in those of the little lamb whose life had ended that day upon the family altar.

And as the King's heart ceased beating, the winged dragons erupted on the scene with a blood-chilling scream of triumph!

David frantically searched the sky for the mighty angels. But they, with their swords sheathed and forgotten, wept and waited at the beams. And as they wept and waited, the King disappeared! In His place there remained but a small shadow...the shadow of a *lamb*!

As the scene faded, another shifted into place before David's eyes. The glistening contour of a throne, the great size of which he was certain had never been seen on earth, emerged where the beams had but a moment before stood.

As David strained to see the mysterious King upon the mystical golden throne, sudden bursts of brilliant color blinded him for a moment!

14

His hands flew to his face to cover his smarting eyes. But with his eyes closed, as though etched upon the inside of his eyelids, the face of the Lamb appeared as well, seated on the throne beside the King! Both wore crowns upon their heads.

And the eyes of the King and the Lamb were the same...

As David slowly opened his own eyes again, only dragons and angels remained. The combat was on! But before a single talon could strike a blow, the angels struck with lightning speed, plunging their swords to the hilts into the loathsome beasts opposing them!

As the dragons gasped in death, the angels danced above them and sang out in triumph,

To Him who sits on the throne
And to the Lamb
Be praise and honor and glory and power,
For ever and ever! Amen![1]

"Snap out of it, kid!" A sharp jab to David's ribs brought him back to reality with a start. "Father's praying! Why can't you pay attention?"

1   Revelation 5:13b.

Chapter Two

WHEN DESTINY CALLS

Five years had passed since the young shepherd boy had seen the King and the Lamb for the first time. Today dawned clear and cool. The wispy clouds floated innocently from west to east, unaware of the drama that had once played out in the night sky over Bethlehem.

Only David had seen it. And the experience had been his rite of passage from childhood to manhood in the space of an instant dream. The boy was now a man—a man whose heart had been forever won by a singular King and a sacrificial Lamb.

The Strange Visit

Zing! Whap! *Reload the sling.* Zing! Whap! *Accuracy is important.* Zing! Whap! *Defend the King!* Zing! Whap! *Slay dragons that war against the Lamb!*

The last stone dropped from the pouch and into his hand. After deftly fitting it snugly within the leather sling, David whirled it around above his head one last time, taking aim at the small circle he had drawn on a distant rock with a piece of charcoal from last night's campfire. Zing! Whap! *Right on target.*

As he unhooked his canteen from his belt to take a drink of water, someone yelled his name from off to the east. Josh, a runner from his father's house, came into view, panting from the fast pace he had kept on the journey to find David.

17

"Come home! Your father wants you!" After stopping ten yards short of David and bending over to get his breath, the lad added with unmistakable excitement, "The Prophet has asked for you! The Prophet!" he repeated breathlessly.

"You mean Samuel? Samuel is at *our* house? Why?" David queried anxiously. "Is Father all right?"

"Sure! Your father's fine! Samuel wants *you*, David! Didn't you hear me?" Josh was getting impatient.

"Yeah, I heard you, but why does he want to see me?" David continued quizzically.

"Who knows? Just c'mon, will you? You're taking forever and everyone's waiting for you! I'll stay with the sheep while you're gone." Josh sank to the ground by David's campfire, which had just expired in the warmth of the morning sun.

David hooked his lyre to his leather belt by securing it with a narrow strap, took a swig of water from the canteen, and set off at a sprint.

"Thanks, Josh," he called over his shoulder to the runner. "Thanks!"

That Night

The house was dark and everyone but David was in bed. Eliab stirred fitfully in his sleep. Only fatigue had overcome his anger at the events of this day. Across the small room, Abinadab sighed softly and closed his eyes. Tomorrow was another day and he'd better get some rest. Life was taking a strange turn, but he must go on living, even if his little brother had been chosen over him, the firstborn, to be the next king of Israel!

Their father, Jesse, was having an unusual dream—a dream of a distant hope somehow fulfilled. He slept deeply.

The Prophet had left after the evening meal. Anointing oil still clung to David's curly hair and simple lambskin tunic.

He couldn't sleep. Leaning against the outside wall of his father's house, David searched the sky for understanding, but the sky remained star-studded and still.

What had Samuel pronounced as he had poured the oil upon his head? King of Israel? Consecrated to rule? How? When? For what purpose? He had no desire for crowns or scepters.

"I am a poet and a sheepherder! What have I to do with such power?" He shrugged his shoulders and ruefully mused about what Israel's present king, Saul, might think of such a prospect!

His attention returned to the sky. No kings or crosses or lambs, not even winged dragons surged across the great expanse above him tonight. Answers remained elusive.

But his heart was drawn—definitely, inexplicably drawn—to the memory of the vision of several years before.

Was he the King he had seen? No, no! To *that* King he would be forever a servant. In an instant of revelation he exclaimed to himself, "Indeed, that King is truly my Lord!" But the heart of the King seemed to be keeping him company.

Was he to be the Lamb? Now there was a question begging an answer. A twinge of pain pricked his heart as he asked, "So I will feel the Lamb's pain?" This seemed certain.

And the crossed beams? What about them? "All that I might ever be must hang upon those rough beams. Power and glory and honor must be dead to me," he whispered, "for they belong forever bound to the King and to the Lamb!" This he also knew.

The night passed with David fixed to the chilled walls of his father's house. As the sky began to lighten in the east, he set out toward the fields to rejoin his sleepy-eyed sheep.

He wanted to leave before the others were awake. His relationship with his brothers seemed now strained and complicated. They would be relieved that he wasn't there when they arose.

As he cleared the outer limits of the town, the very song that his mind had been chasing five years ago just as he was summoned to the evening sacrifice fell gently, effortlessly into place! He sang it as though he had known it for a lifetime, but softly only for the Lamb to hear as he searched the sky again for some sign of his Lord, the King.

The melody floated upward, carried by the early morning breezes and drawn ever higher by the rays of the rising sun.

> *I wait for the Lord,*
> *My soul waits;*
> *In His Word*
> *I put my hope.*
> *My soul waits for the Lord*
> *More than watchmen*
> *Wait for the morning,*
> *More than watchmen*
> *Wait for the morning.*
>
> *My heart is not proud,*
> *My eyes are not haughty.*
> *My hope is in the Lord*
> *Now and forevermore.*[1]

---

1   Adapted from Psalm 130:5-6; 131:1a,3.

Chapter Three

UNDER THE ANOINTING

Something was in the wind. The sheep could smell it and were stirring restlessly, agitated and nearing the point of panic. David's eyes peered through the twilight, studying each bush and rock and scrubby desert tree for a sign of the intruder. So far, nothing gave its presence away but the scent picked up by the sheep.

After building up the campfire to a stalwart blaze, he ranged among the sheep gathering and carrying the weakest of them to places nearer the fire. Whatever was out there would not like the flames.

Suddenly a ram near the northern edge of the flock bolted in fright at a growing figure in the distance. In a matter of seconds, he had started a stampede, but with every lamb running in a different direction! It was chaos!

"All right," pronounced David to himself, "this is what all the slingshot practice has been about. Whatever this beast is, it will meet its match tonight!"

With that, David took off in the direction of the now encroaching shadow, pulling out his sling and tucking a stone into it as he ran. Adrenaline surged through his body as he neared the beast, which was preparing to charge a fat sheep that hadn't been able to keep up with the rest.

Closer now, David could make out the nature of the predator. It was a lion, a huge male lion with lips curled in a snarl that revealed gleaming white teeth aimed at the chubby prey before it.

Round and round above his head the sturdy shepherd swung his sling.

Just as the lion was about to spring upon the sheep, it caught sight of its pursuer! But before it could shift direction and charge David instead, David released the stone from its sling with lightning speed. The missile struck the lion in the head with a resounding thud, knocking the beast back onto its haunches.

But the fight was far from over and David knew it. Face to face they came, the lion stunned but furious and David filled with a superhuman power he had never felt before.

Without giving it a thought, David fell upon the lion, grabbing its jaws and stretching them painfully wide, one in each hand, twisting the lion's neck until he heard it snap! In one great spasm of agony, the lion flailed its front feet wildly, its claws slashing David's left side and thigh.

In but a moment, the battle ceased. The lion lay heaving its last breath there in the sand at David's feet.

New Understanding

As David bent down to wash his wounds in the stream, he noticed something new in the eyes of his own reflection in the still water. Where had he seen that look before?

A scene from the nearly-forgotten vision fixed itself before him like a giant still-life painting. The *King on the crossed beams* had worn that look! He could see it now clearly. Had risking his life for his sheep produced that look of compassion? Had he really come to love them that much?

Later as he was moving the flock away from the scene of the fray, he realized that a power from somewhere beyond himself had fought that battle. The Spirit of the God of his people, the God whom he had loved since early childhood when his father had first told him stories of how Jehovah had delivered his ancestors from their enemies time after time, had given him strength.

God was with him! *That*, in fact, was what had begun the day Samuel had visited him and prayed for him. He had not been able to put his finger on what had transpired that night until now.

And God was somehow one with the King of his vision! This he knew as surely as he knew his own name! It was beginning to make sense. *God's* hand was upon him. It was no accident.

As this revelation settled upon young David, he reverently dropped to his knees and then stretched out upon the ground, his face in the dust. That night he learned to worship the God he loved as the King he would serve all the days of his life.

In His Presence

How long he lay there on the ground he didn't know, but when he arose, the sun was well up into the sky and the sheep needed tending.

Refreshed in his spirit by those hours in God's presence, he found a new song rising from his heart. As he rounded up the strays and led them to water, words and music tumbled from his mouth. The song was of today, but also somehow of days yet to come:

Who is God besides the Lord?
And who is the Rock except our God?
It is God who arms me with strength
And makes my way perfect.

He makes my feet like the feet of a deer;
He enables me to stand on the heights.
He trains my hands for battle;
My arms can bend a bow of bronze.

The Lord lives! Praise be to my Rock!
Exalted be God my Savior!
He gives His king great victories;
He shows unfailing kindness to His anointed,
To David and His descendants forever.[1]

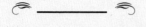

1   Psalm 18:31-34,46,50.

Chapter Four

THE TORTURED KING

"The ticks are awful this year," David declared more to himself than to the ram he was doctoring at the moment. *It's a wonder this big guy hasn't gone out of his mind with these things burrowing around under his skin.* The young shepherd shuddered involuntarily at the thought.

With one hand pouring the oil, tar, and herb concoction from a sheepskin flask onto the head of the distraught sheep, David's other hand gently massaged the mixture into all the sores and red areas where the ticks had made their entrance.

The ears were especially infested. "So that's why you haven't been listening so well to me lately, big fella," said David as he swabbed the healing balm in and around the ram's velvety ears. "You know if you'd not spend so much time trying to forge your own path through the brambles at the pasture's edge, you'd not be in such a mess! Why can't you trust me to get you to good food?" At this the ram tossed back his head and let out an ornery bleat that made even David jump!

"All right, all right! Have it your way! If you want pain, you'll get pain!" Then sadly David asked the stubborn beast before him, "Why won't you ever learn?"

The Strange Invitation

The day passed quickly as David administered the mixture to lamb after lamb. And just as he was washing himself at sunset in the stream that meandered through the valley, he spotted a figure in the distance, coming his way.

It was his brother Eliab, looking annoyed as well as tired from his day-long trek from Bethlehem. Pouches of fresh provisions—bread, cheese, dates, and nuts—hung from his right shoulder. Tied to his back was his bedroll.

What could he want? David mused. *Why hasn't Father sent a servant with the food instead?*

The answer was made clear as soon as they were within earshot of one another. Eliab was not interested in chatting at any length with his kid brother, so he got right to the point.

"I'm taking your place for a few days. Get some sleep. You're leaving in the morning," Eliab tersely announced. After dumping the supplies unceremoniously at David's campsite and throwing his tired body down onto a patch of soft grass nearby, he continued, "King Saul is having one of his 'spells' again and has called for you and your stupid music! For some reason he thinks it'll help him sleep. He really must be crazy!"

Pleased at his own cleverness, Eliab glanced at his little brother and laughed.

At the sound of his laughter, several of the sheep reacted with a cacophony of baa's, which made David laugh this time. *Even they know what a grouch my brother is!* he said to himself.

"Don't they ever shut up?" retorted Eliab in response to the fresh outbreak of noise.

Ignoring his question, David softly began reflecting in a quiet voice about Israel's new king. "Nobody knows what's wrong with him, I guess. They say that ever since that episode at Gilgal—when he got scared and acted in the place of Samuel the prophet in offering the sacrifice—he's not been the same. I heard that Samuel was really upset with him, and no wonder. He disobeyed God Himself!" David said with awe in his voice.

"Well, whatever," grunted Eliab with a shrug of his shoulders. "All I know is that one minute he's a heroic warrior, and the next he's so full of fear he goes crazy! What a mess!"

David cut off two liberal hunks of cheese, one of which he gave to his brother who by now was sitting up and drinking thirstily from his sheepskin canteen. Taking the cheese, Eliab muttered, "You'll get to see it all firsthand! That's an experience I'd rather not have. I hate tending sheep, but I'd prefer being out here in no man's land to being trapped in the same room with a lunatic!"

In silence, they finished the cheese and followed it with two slices of their mother's freshly baked bread, each lost in his own thoughts for a few minutes.

After wiping his mouth on the sleeve of his tunic, Eliab spread his bedroll out on the patch of grass where he had been sitting and prepared to turn in for the night. David put the provisions securely away and made one last round of checking the sheep before settling down on his own bedroll.

About to fall asleep, Eliab yawned and made his final comment on David's upcoming adventure. "Good luck, kid. You're gonna need it." He almost felt sorry for David.

The Nightmare

As David drifted off to sleep, visions of earthly kings played about his head.

Then one of the kings grew bigger and bigger, until all the others fled!

The eyes of this foreboding king bore into David's soul as he slept. He could almost feel the king's breath in his face as he came closer and closer.

"God, help me!" he cried out in his dream.

Restlessly, David tossed and turned, soundlessly crying out again, "Please, God, help me!" In but a moment the grip of the nightmare was broken, much as a fever breaks in the night, and the entire vision faded away.

All that remained were the strains of a haunting melody which slowly seeped into his soul as he slept deeply, at peace.

I love the Lord
For He heard my voice,
He heard my cry for mercy.
Ah, because He turned His ear to me,
I will call on Him as long as I live,
As long as I live![1]

1   Adapted from Psalm 116:1-2.

Chapter Five

WHEN GIANTS ROAR

David's trips to the palace to play and sing for the king were frequent that first year and often extended. Each time he played for King Saul the effect was the same: As the gentle songs that he had composed for his sheep fell upon the ears of the tormented king, the wild, frenzied, and fearful look in Saul's eyes subsided and sense returned.

The young sheepherder sang of dreams and kings and mystical things, of powers in Heaven and worship on earth. He sang of sorrow and suffering, of forgiveness and mercy, and the sad king would sigh and fall asleep. Over and over the scene was replayed. The bond grew between sufferer and singer.

The king was an enigma to his servants and even his family. But to David it mattered only that he was the King of Israel, chosen by God, to be honored for the authority vested in him, no matter what his present malady. David loved the king, and his loyalty endeared him to everyone at court.

War in the Wind

But as spring approached, he was summoned less often. King Saul and his men were suiting up for battle against the Philistine forces, their ever-present and powerful enemies to the west. There was going to be war this year for sure.

David's brothers—Eliab, Abinadab, and Shammah—had caught the "battle fever" along with thousands of other young men of military age, and had enlisted in the army.

By late spring the battle lines were drawn in the Valley of Elah. The Philistines occupied the hill on one side of the valley and the Israelites occupied the hill on the opposite side. They would meet in the middle of the valley for the conflict.

But things had turned strange; the Philistines had produced a mammoth of a man as their champion, and instead of the two armies meeting in mass combat, the Philistines were insisting that only their giant and a representative from the Israelite army must engage in a fight. The outcome would determine slavehood of one nation to the other, the loser to the victor.

The giant, Goliath from Gath, was nine feet tall! His head was protected by a bronze helmet and his body by a coat of scale armor of bronze weighing 125 pounds. A bronze javelin was slung on his back. So enormous was the shaft of his spear that it could be likened to a weaver's rod, its iron point alone weighing 15 pounds!

The Israelites, having no such man of comparable size or strength, literally quaked in their sandals wondering what to do to fend off this formidable foe! Day after day, for 40 long days, King Saul and his men retreated from the line of battle when Goliath challenged them to combat, defying them to their faces.

The Mission

Back in Bethlehem, David's father called him from the fields. Jesse was deeply concerned about his elder sons' safety and longed for word from them. He instructed David to carry food to his brothers and a gift of cheeses to the commander of their unit, and then return with a report on their welfare.

30

Early the next morning, after leaving his flock in the care of another shepherd, David loaded up his father's donkey and set off for the battlefield.

At the Scene

The adrenaline pumped through David's body as he traveled as quickly as he could with the supplies to the Valley of Elah. Would he see King Saul? Was the king well? Had he anyone to sing for him on the battlefield?

"Enough of such thoughts! There's a battle to be fought and a war to be won, and I might even get to see some of the action!" David chided himself aloud.

"The only thing I don't understand is why the conflict is being so dragged out. What's the holdup?" By now David's stride was long and his face set with determination to get some answers. He was through being a child.

As he crested the last hill, the Valley of Elah lay before him, and what he saw astounded him. Two mighty armies had positioned themselves on either side, one boisterous and jaunty, each man shaking his fist in the air, and the other huddled in a motionless lump. When the battle cry went up, both armies ran to their battle lines, one still defiant, the other intimidated and bewildered.

David hurried into the Israelite camp where he left the supplies with a steward, and then ran to find his brothers at the front line. The silence among the Israelite troops was eerie, and it was the silence that propelled David into the conflict.

The events of the next 60 minutes were a blur to David: Goliath's taunt against God's people, King Saul's promises of reward, impossible armor, slings, stones, swords, blood.

That Night

His own words rang in his ears long into the night following his felling of the giant and the slaughter of the enemy.

From somewhere deep inside himself he had shouted to Goliath, "You come against me with sword and spear and javelin, but I come against you in the name of the Lord Almighty, the God of the armies of Israel, whom you have defied. This day the Lord will hand you over to me, and I'll strike you down and cut off your head...and the whole world will know that there is a God in Israel. All those gathered here will know that it is not by sword or spear that the Lord saves; for the battle is the Lord's, and He will give all of you into our hands!"

And then around and around he had swung his sling with that single smooth stone in it. Swiftly and surely it had found its mark between the eyes of the giant. How the ground had shaken at his fall! And how the people had cheered him!

"But why this mad celebration of my deed?" he had asked, bewildered by their extravagant praise of him. "*God* guided my hand and secured this victory!"

He had wanted to shout this fact from the mountaintops until every Israelite got the message.

Now as he lay uneasily on his bedroll in one of King Saul's tents he wondered aloud, "How could it have been otherwise? How could I *not* have won the conflict against an enemy of God?"

Unable to Sleep

David rose in the darkness and paced back and forth in the sand outside the tent where he was staying until released to return to his sheep.

"Is it this dark temptation to take God's credit that drives men to madness? Does being worshiped birth insanity? Is it the fear of losing that worship, once enjoyed, that haunts my lord, King Saul?

"What's to become of such a man?" David whispered into the air as he sank wearily back down onto his bed.

There would be no dreams nor songs nor sleep tonight.

Chapter Six

DODGING SPEARS

David awoke with a start.

Watch out! Move! Duck! Dodge! His body jerked this way and that as he struggled to avoid the spears of the mad king whom he loved. Beads of sweat popped out on his forehead and his linen tunic stuck to his body.

Then, as he gained full consciousness, to his relief he saw not the haunted eyes of King Saul, but silver stars against a black velvet sky framed by his bedroom window.

He was alone. It had been a bad dream.

Uncertain Times

The trips into Gibeah to play and sing for the king had ended at Goliath's death. Saul had refused to let him return home. David was given a small house near the palace so that he could be on call at all hours of the day and night.

It was the uncertainty that was most distressing. In what mood would King Saul be when David was summoned? Sometimes Saul welcomed him like a son and shared his heart with the young shepherd-turned-warrior. At those times the haunted, melancholy moods seemed a distant memory. But at other times he ranted and raved about power and destiny and the hatred in his soul for anyone who would steal his glory.

At those times King Saul's gaze would inevitably turn to fix upon David, the chant sung by the women after Goliath's defeat pounding in his ears:

Saul has slain his thousands
And David, his tens of thousands!

And the spears would fly.

But always, when the fever of fear and jealousy was spent and the spear was stuck fast in the wall by David's head, sanity returned and Saul was sorry for his fury. He would slump back upon his couch and say, "Play, David, play," with sadness filling his eyes...but never freedom.

Hard Questions

With a moan, David forced himself out of bed and over to the brass stand on which rested a pitcher of water and an ornate basin for washing. After emptying the contents of the pitcher into the basin, he proceeded to splash the water onto his sweaty face.

The shock of the cold water against his hot flesh erased the last illusions of sleep and helped dislodge the dream that had come in the night.

"King of Israel! Could not prophets and priests have been enough? Did Abraham, Isaac, or Jacob ever dream of kingship?" David wondered. "Not likely," the young shepherd concluded as he dried his face with a soft linen towel.

"What agony they avoided!" declared David, shaking his head to fully clear the nightmare from his mind.

Uncomfortable in the close quarters of this little room, David climbed the stairs in the corner that led to the rooftop. There, at last, he could breathe freely.

But then, as he looked down upon the city below and present reality came into focus—quite apart from dreams and nightmares—a cold chill settled into his heart. And the questions he had long been avoiding stole up from that chill, pressing themselves uneasily upon his mind: Will I too throw spears to keep the throne? *Will I also lose my sanity when the crown descends upon my head? Will I grasp authority that belongs to God alone? Will I kill friends and slaughter innocents in my delusions?*

With his face in his hands, the future monarch fell to his knees on the gravel floor of the rooftop and wept.

"O God, save me from myself! I long only for Your Presence! If I must be king someday, keep me from arrogance. Search me continually to see if there is any wicked way in me! O God, lead me, lead me in the way that is everlasting and righteous, for You alone are my King and my God!"

As comfort swept his soul in answer to the cry of his heart, peace returned.

After a time, an older and wiser David rose and stretched his arms toward the sky.

Remembering

Returning to his room below, David placed a comfortable, high-backed chair in front of the open window, facing it. He reached for his lyre, settling it snugly within the crook of one arm. With the fingers of his other hand, he gently strummed the strings.

Looking out into the night, he pretended that he was back under the stars with his sheep. And there within the gates of Saul's stronghold, David worshiped his God, the true King of the crossed beams of his vision so long ago.

You, O Lord,
Are a shield about me,
You're my glory,
And the lifter of my head![1]

1   Adapted from Psalm 3:3.

Over and over David sang this simple song to his heavenly King. And as the sky began to lighten in the east, his thoughts were far away.

Had it not been for Goliath, he would be fixing himself a breakfast of dates, bread, and cheese at this very moment. And then, after a long draught of water from the stream, he would scout around among the youngest lambs for one he hadn't carried recently. Picking it up and cradling it gently but firmly in his left arm, and grabbing his staff with his right, he would hold it fast while rounding up stragglers and prodding the lazy. It would be time by now to find fresh pasture downstream.

And what would he be singing for all the sheep, rocks, and hills to hear?

Strangely, as he asked himself this last question, the words and melody of a new song stole into his spirit. He sang it hesitantly:

> *Praise be to the Lord,*
> *For He has heard my cry!*
> *The Lord is my strength and shield*
> *My heart trusts in Him!*
>
> *Save Your people and bless them!*
> *Be their shepherd*
> *And in Your arms carry them*
> *Forever, O Lord!*[2]

David stood, his lyre still cradled in his arm, and looked once again down upon the city outside his window.

"Our sheep have become the two-legged kind," he sighed and then smiled, ever so slightly.

2   Adapted from Psalm 28:6-7,9.

Chapter Seven

WHEN DOUBTS RAGE

No matter what David did for the king, he did it well. Before long, Saul gave him a high rank in the army, which greatly pleased everyone. But as David's heroism increased, Saul's jealously likewise increased. The brooding king began plotting daily David's demise.

But nothing worked for Saul; he could not kill David himself because of David's popularity, nor could he undo the young warrior by sending him into the thick of battle. For ten years, no matter what David set his sword to in the service of the king, he succeeded and remained unharmed. From battle after bloody battle, David returned victorious. To Saul's chagrin, David even won the king's daughter Michal in marriage after a particularly fierce conflict with the Philistines.

Precious Friends

All of Israel loved him, especially Saul's own son Jonathan. It seemed that the more Saul hated David, the stronger grew Jonathan's defense of him. But when the spears also began to fly at Jonathan, and members of his own household were ordered to kill him, David knew that his uneasy liaison with the king had come to an end and he must flee once and for all. Jonathan knew that as well and had made it very clear.

As they met in the safety of a remote desert spot to seal the decision, David had questions.

"What have I done, Jonathan, to deserve such hatred?" David searched his young friend's eyes for a sane answer. But there was none.

"I swear, I have no designs on his throne! You know I have asked for nothing from him. Instead, I have risked my life again and again to preserve his throne *for* him! Is he blind?" an exasperated David asked Jonathan as they huddled over a small fire, trying to warm themselves on that cold day in the desert.

After several minutes Jonathan caught David's eye and began answering him very carefully.

"David, my father is frantic," he said with sad intensity. "He is no fool; he knows that the Spirit of God that rested on him years ago now rests on you. While his mind contrives ways to persevere without the anointing, his spirit knows that it cannot last. For whatever reason, he simply finds it impossible to trust God."

Dropping his head and breaking eye contact with David, Jonathan spoke in little more than a whisper, "I don't remember him ever *trusting* God."

"Is that why he disobeyed God and offered that sacrifice, all those years ago, that cost him God's blessing?" David asked quietly.

Shifting his weight a bit, Jonathan looked hard at David once again. "Yes, that and because his fear of men and what they thought of him was much greater than his fear of God," he concluded.

"And what about you, Jonathan? You're next in line for the throne. If God intends me to be king and your father presses me to combat, don't you fear for your own life—if not from me, from someone who attempts to promote me to the throne in your place?" They had needed to talk about this, but it was not easy.

Jonathan stood erect and his eyes searched the sky as though for confirmation of his answer.

"I'm not like my father, David," he slowly and deliberately pronounced. "I trust God. I want what He wants! *He is God and I am not.*"

Clearing his throat and wiping his eyes with the back of his hand, he continued, "If I must die to bring the leadership He wants over His people, so be it. I am no contender. I have not been anointed; I will trust the Prophet on that issue. All I ask is that you deal kindly with my family after I am gone."

This left David speechless.

A Rare Quality

"My friend," Jonathan spoke tenderly to David, just above a whisper, "I love you because you love my father even though he hates you. You have taught me loyalty even in a violent home—a lesson that I will have to remember after you leave and I return to serve my father."

Jonathan continued, his voice filled with conviction, "But I love you much, much more because you love God more dearly than you love yourself. That is a rare quality in men these days!"

After a pause in which he turned to face David, "You will rule wisely, my friend." At that, Jonathan and David embraced.

Now weeping, David begged, "But Jonathan, you must pray for me! Like you, I know that I am not God. I will surely make mistakes; I will not always be wise! Will you still love me then?" David pressed for consolation.

"Yes, as will God. Just be wise enough to repent, my dear friend. Always, be that wise."

The Test

The wind blew hard against the forms of the two friends who separated that night. Jonathan, with the wind full in his face, returned breathless and sad to his father's house.

David, with the wind pressing against his back, let that wind drive him deeper into the wilderness that would soon become his new home.

Along the way, tired and hungry, he stopped at Nob and, by lying, secured bread and Goliath's sword from Ahimelech the priest. David told the priest that he was on a special mission for the king and that, since it was to be kept a secret, no one should know that he had been there. Assuming the king's approval, Ahimelech granted his request for the sword and the bread.

But in the act of obtaining what he wanted under false pretenses, the testing of David's soul began.

It was as though the Philistine's sword and the ill-gotten bread had a power all their own to entice him. He sought shelter in Gath, Goliath's hometown, and found himself at the gate to King Achish's palace. What insanity!

And insanity is what he feigned. In fear that the servants would attack him thinking him an enemy, David pretended he was crazy, making strange marks on the gate and drooling!

For the first time in his life David sought the fever that had driven Saul mad. And it secured his freedom. Even the enemy refused to consort with a lunatic! In disgust, they threw him out, unharmed.

Facing Himself

Alone that night in the cave of Adullam, David groaned before God in misery. "How, God, can I be your anointed? What a mockery I am!" Beating his breast, he wept and wept.

"Is it true that I can so easily be like Saul?" he asked himself, weakness suddenly overcoming him, causing his legs to buckle beneath him.

"My God, how could I have dragged Your glory through the dirt at the feet of unholy men?" At this, the weeping began afresh.

There in the cave, prostrate before the God he loved, David repented. He remained on his face until his spirit cleared.

Then quietly he rose and brushed himself off. Removing the bedroll from his back, he made it ready for the night. There was no need for food. If he never ate again, it would not matter.

He had faced himself...and God had won.

Chapter Eight

DESERT EXILE

The days of leading great armies into glorious battle seemed to be from the life of someone else. David gave them little thought now. He would just as soon be alone.

However, from time to time he shared a meal with a shepherd who happened to be in one of the pastures that ranged along the eastern border of King Saul's domain. How comforting to be among the sheep again, even if they weren't his own. But at each encounter, he was careful not to reveal his true identity.

The young fugitive knew, however, that before long he would be found. Whether by friend or foe, he would surely be found.

Meanwhile, in the precious days and nights of solitude David composed mystical melodies to the Lamb of his vision long ago. He and God met in these moments of truth and became bound to one another at the heart. And the fear of man that could have yet turned feigned insanity into the real thing, left him permanently.

The dreams were few those days. But a strange sense of destiny began to haunt David. It was "strange" because the destiny never seemed to be completely his. He was somehow just a part of it. What did God intend for him, David wondered, that he could only partly live it out in his own lifetime?

Surprise in the Dark

One particularly cold night, when the campfire he had built at the mouth of the cave blazed cheerily and should have coaxed him to sleep, David found sleep impossible. In the flames he began to see what looked like dragons' breath—shards of fiery air shooting this way and that.

"Ah, now this is an exciting story for a dreary night," David said aloud with a laugh. Directing himself to the imaginary dragons, he playfully asked, "And what are you guys chasing there in my fire?" Hoping to see that the prey was more of the same—ugly creatures that he'd take delight in seeing devour one another—David strained to make out their shapes in the inferno.

Then suddenly the hair on the back of David's neck stood out and a chill ran down his spine. Unable to help himself, David let out a startled cry! There was someone behind him, in the deeper recesses of the cave!

Grabbing the stout club that he always kept beside his bedroll at night, David sprang to his feet and whirled around to meet the intruder. With legs bent slightly like coiled springs, his left arm cocked with its hand in a fist and his right arm swinging the club above his head, he inched his way toward the figure he sensed hidden in the dark.

Whack! Something slammed into his left thigh, sending shooting pain up to his waist and down to his ankle. To keep from losing his balance, David lowered his club to help steady himself, dropping his guard for a moment.

Ooof! A fist intersected with one of his ribs, at chest level.

David instinctively swung with his left fist, hitting what felt like a bearded jaw. A sharp cry of pain followed. Tossing the club away from himself and his antagonist, David's right hand was now free as well.

44

Wham! A direct hit to the dark figure's stomach, at which he doubled over, gasping for breath. Pressing his advantage, David grabbed him by his clothing and hurled him nearer the fire, trying to get him to a place where he could see what manner of man he was fighting.

Not giving up, his opponent struggled to his feet. With a guttural roar, he lunged at David and swung again, missing David's jaw by at least a foot.

Gaining the Upper Hand

In an instant, David had the moving figure in a headlock, his right arm quickly tightening its position around the stranger's neck. Choking and gasping for breath, the defeated foe managed to spit out, "I surrender!" as David dropped the limp form to the ground.

Staring down at him, David demanded, "Who are you? What are you doing here? Are you alone?" Getting no answers, David threateningly held his fist before the man's face. "You want more of this, do you?"

"No, no," he managed. Clearing his throat, the rough-hewn man spoke again, "I'm hiding here from the king's thugs. I'm not looking for any trouble!"

"Are you alone?" David pressed.

Sitting up and rubbing his jaw, "Yeah, I'm alone. And that's the way I want it." Then, looking at David with fear behind his eyes he asked anxiously, "You aren't going to tell anyone you found me, are you?"

David, relaxing a bit now that the crisis was obviously past, eased his sore body down to the ground a few feet away and answered somewhat sheepishly, "Not if you don't tell anyone you found *me*."

Their eyes met and an understanding passed between them. Although still a bit guarded, they both let out a laugh.

Later, as the two fugitives bedded down to catch what sleep they could before dawn, imaginary angels felled dragons in the dancing flames of their campfire.

Chapter Nine

SAD REGRET

The number of his followers grew almost daily as word spread among the discontented and those outlawed by King Saul—in debt to the government or to society—that David was alive and well in the desert. They came alone and they came in small bands—renegade soldiers, thieves, and murderers. Some were unjustly accused, others deserved every invective ever hurled at them by those they had wronged. All wanted to be with David, who had become something of a folk hero to them.

Even his parents and brothers sought him out. But, as Eliab was quick to sarcastically point out, it was not because being on the run with him was so alluring, but because their lives were worth nothing now that David was out of favor with the king! His family was being terrorized.

While the others slept that night, Eliab cornered David.

"You owe us, kid," Eliab said in a forced whisper, through clenched teeth. "Our property has been seized and our flocks slaughtered, all because of you and your 'anointing'!"

David said nothing, only his eyes registering the misery of the moment.

"What a laugh!" Eliab muttered in derision. "King of Israel! Well, ol' Saul's got your number, and it'll soon be up, as I see it."

Still David said nothing.

"Look at the way you're living! The son of Jesse, a cave dweller and vagabond! And now we've been reduced to the same lot!" Eliab's anger mounted.

Without a word David took his brother firmly by the shoulders and pulled him suddenly toward himself until their faces were only inches apart. This surprised Eliab, checking his anger for the moment.

Finally David spoke. "Eliab, I'm sorry," he said in a hoarse whisper. "I'm sorry you've gotten dragged into my grief. I would never have wished it upon you." As he finished speaking, he gently released his brother.

Then nodding toward his worn and exhausted mother and father who were asleep on a mat in a corner of the cave a few yards away, "Last night I spoke with the king of Moab about them. He is a compassionate man. He has consented to taking Mother and Father into his home for protection," David continued in a whisper so as not to wake them. "I'll take them to Mizpah in the morning."

Eliab shot back, "What about the rest of us?"

"That's up to you," David said matter-of-factly. "You are welcome to stay here with me, or you can set out on your own."

Eliab sat stiffly, trying to think.

"Life takes some strange twists sometimes, doesn't it?" David reflected quietly. "Our God's plans are often beyond our understanding."

"Leave God out of this!" Eliab seethed.

His eyes wet with tears, David said softly, "I can't."

At David's reply, Eliab grabbed his bedroll and knapsack and stormed out of the cave.

He did not return.

Courage and Comradery

Each day, to relieve boredom and to prepare for possible combat with Saul's troops, David drilled his band of misfits, which now numbered four hundred. They must be in prime physical condition; able to fight hard without faltering; loyal to one another to the death, if necessary; full of spirit; and highly skilled in their weaponry. David was a relentless master at shaping a military force; he had had much practice at it as a leader of vast forces under King Saul.

They became protectors of sheepherders and their flocks against marauders, and of villages within Judah against Philistine invaders. In return, they were given food and plunder.

They were continually moving from one desert stronghold to another to evade Saul and his men.

But at night, no matter where they were, they begged David for music. Sometimes he made up jolly tunes that made them laugh, but mostly he taught them of the love and faithfulness of God through the poignant verses he so easily set to music.

When David bared his soul in praise and worship of his beloved heavenly King, the men were drawn irresistibly to seek Him as well. It was contagious—this love of David for His God—and it spread through the hearts of his men, bringing many to repentance for their past sins.

And the men loved David. He cared for them as a shepherd would care for his sheep. To a man, they knew that he would lay his life down for them. They knew that he considered them first when he made decisions. They knew that he was straight with them; so they were straight with him.

Sad Discovery

"David, there's a guy outside who wants to see you," whispered Ben, one of the lookouts, rousing David in the middle of the night. "I guess he's a priest or something. He's carrying a strange-looking vest that one of the men says is an 'ephod.' "

After sitting up quickly and rubbing the sleep from his eyes, David stretched briefly and replied, "Tell him to wait with you outside. I'll be right there." David grabbed his tunic and sword and prepared to meet his guest.

The night visitor was Abiathar, whose father was Ahimelech, the priest at Nob from whom David had secured bread and Goliath's sword many months before. David had since been deeply ashamed that he had deceived Ahimelech by saying he was on a mission for Saul, when in reality he was running from Saul. He had put the priest in a very compromising position by tricking him into giving him what he wanted.

And the worst, David now discovered, had come to pass.

"David, that day there had been a spy in the village. He saw you and reported to King Saul that my father had given you aid," Abiathar's voice broke.

"Go on," David urged gently. "What happened? Is your father all right?" he asked anxiously.

"He's dead! When the king's men wouldn't touch a priest, he ordered Doeg, the slimy spy, to kill him!"

David put his arms around Abiathar, who was by now sobbing.

"And it didn't stop there! All 85 priests of Nob and every living soul in the village, as well as their livestock, were put to the sword! I alone escaped!" At this the young man completely broke down in David's arms.

"What kind of an animal could do such a thing, David? And what am I to do? Doeg saw me run!" Panic seized Abiathar and he trembled.

"Shh," David said soothingly. "You're going to be all right. I want you to stay with me, if you will have me."

Then, with great pain in his voice, David added, "But perhaps you won't want to be with me, Abiathar." Clearing his throat, David continued, "You see, it is my fault that everyone died! If I had told your father that I was running from Saul, he could have refused me. I am responsible!"

The boy was stunned! Pain and disbelief filled his eyes, while the sight tore at David's heart.

"If you can forgive me, please stay," David pleaded. "Even if you can't forgive me, please stay and allow me to protect you from your pursuers," David urged, searching the boy's face for understanding.

"You see," said David sadly, "my enemies have inescapably become your enemies as well."

Abiathar stayed. That night while the lad slept in safety among David's mighty men, David paced the desert sand and grieved.

Chapter Ten

MERCY AND HONOR

Davids's songs became a private cry to God during those days of Saul's hot pursuit of his life. On certain nights he sang alone:

> *Deliver me from my enemies, O God;*
> *Protect me from those who rise up against me.*
>
> *Deliver me from evildoers*
> *And save me from bloodthirsty men!*
>
> *Refrain: Have mercy on me, O God,*
> *Have mercy on me,*
> *For in You my soul takes refuge.*
> *I will take refuge in the shadow of Your wings*
> *Until the disaster has passed.*[1]

The Chase

"He's gone now, David!" Josiah called, running up to him as they stopped for water on their way to the Desert of En Gedi to hide from Saul.

"The king was so close you could almost feel his breath on our necks! He and his army were right over on the other

☞ ——— ☜

1   Psalm 59:1-2; 57:1.

side of that hill!" He pointed excitedly to the hill not a quarter of a mile away.

"But we faked him out, didn't we?" the young man continued breathlessly.

"Calm down, my friend," said David with a sad smile, laying his hand on the young man's shoulder to help settle him. "It's not over yet. He'll be back!"

Stooping to splash cold water on his grimy face, David corrected Josiah. "Actually, Saul left of his own accord. He has more pressing matters to attend to...the Philistines are raiding his towns."

Handing Josiah a water jug, David said, "Here, fill this and then thank God for your safety!"

His young friend persisted, "But I wish we were fighting them right now! I'm ready, David, really I am!" He tried to reassure David. "The men all want to fight...*now*!"

Not knowing when to stop, Josiah continued. "I'm sick of running and I'd like to slice that ol' army and their leader up into little pieces!" At this, Josiah brandished his sword in the air, swishing it from side to side with a flourish.

"Josiah! You forget who the enemy is! In the front of that army marches the anointed King of Israel! Do you think taking the sword to him is a small matter to God?" David was grimly serious now.

David continued, making sure Josiah was listening. "We will defend ourselves *from* him, but God save us from ever taking his life intentionally," he said with finality.

Young Josiah dropped his bravado under these strong words from the man he so loved and admired. He would do nothing to risk David's disapproval and was now a bit embarrassed.

"Yes, sir. I'm sorry, David." He quickly filled the jug and hurried away. But underneath his submission lay hidden a great difficulty in understanding the battle plans of this, his future king.

David's Chance

As David had predicted to Josiah, Saul indeed resumed pursuit after subduing the Philistines. It was in the Desert of En Gedi that their paths crossed again.

Unaware that David was anywhere nearby, Saul unwittingly entered, unattended, the very cave in which David's men were hiding! As they saw him enter, they held their breaths and beckoned to David to attack.

David didn't move a muscle, his body frozen in indecision. But as Saul moved about the cave, with his back to the hidden men, David's fingers tightened their grip on his spear.

Suddenly his thoughts flashed back to another time and another place. He and Saul were in the palace, and it was Saul who was holding the spear.

Fear shot through David's heart...and then for one intense moment, a new emotion fought to rule. A fiery, fierce desire for revenge pressed him from every side! Like a hot coal, the spear burned in his hand, taunting him, urging him to act.

No! he screamed soundlessly to himself. *Never will I pass judgment on God's anointed! Never!*

And the fever passed.

Instead, David cut off a corner of the robe Saul had tossed nearby, and even then regretted doing that.

After Saul had rejoined his men outside, David emerged as well, holding aloft the soft, red fabric of the king's robe.

"I could have killed you in there, my lord. It would have been so easy! But I will never lay a hand on you to harm you," David shouted.

Saul, completely taken by surprise, stood there with his mouth agape at the sight of David.

Then lowering his voice but not its intensity, David asked, "But why do you stalk me like an animal? I am guilty only of faithful service to you, never rebellion! Why do you treat me this way?"

At this, Saul seemed to come to his senses...and for the moment his fever, too, passed. He repented and headed back home.

Vulnerable Again

But his repentance was short-lived. Some weeks later, on a chilly, windless night, David and his men happened upon Saul and his army camped beside the road on the hill of Hakilah, as they were again pursuing David's life. Saul and Abner, his commander, were asleep in the camp, the army in a wide circle around them.

Pulses pounding, David and Abishai sneaked through the encirclement and into the camp, totally undetected!

How poorly his men protect him, the King of Israel! What a disgrace! David thought to himself, indignantly.

Abishai had other thoughts on his mind.

"Today God has truly delivered your enemy into your hands," he whispered to David as they stealthily crept up to where Saul was sleeping, the king's spear stuck in the ground near his head.

"Now let me pin him to the ground with one thrust of the spear," plotted Abishai, his pulse pounding with excitement. "I won't need to strike him twice!"

Weary from months of being hunted, for a moment David could imagine the spear penetrating Saul's heart, setting him free at last from the hound that perpetually nipped at his heels. Surely all Israel would receive him as king if this madman were finally out of the way. It made so much sense.

Divine Intervention

But just as the temptation began to play with his mind, David's vision strangely blurred. Within seconds, he couldn't see a thing! All was blackness, like the velvet blackness of a starless night.

As he strained fiercely to see Saul and Abner who lay at his feet, only eyes appeared before him—the eyes of the Lamb and of the Shepherd King of his dreams! David broke out in a cold sweat.

From those eyes in the night sky shot dreadful looks of warning that burned all the way through David's body to his very heart. Then his vision became clear again.

Quickly grabbing hold of Abishai's arm, David held him back. "No! Don't do it! You can't kill him! That's not why we came down here!"

Abishai stared at David in disbelief. "But this is your chance! If you don't kill him, he'll surely kill you!" he pleaded.

Then, in an exasperated and hoarse whisper, Abishai made one last appeal. "David, do this deed, or let me do it for you, and be done with this infernal insanity!"

David's eyes, now full of fire, locked onto Abishai's and held them fast. "Only God has the authority to decide the day and manner of this man's death. He will take care of it."

Saul stirred slightly. "Now, get the spear and water jug that are near his head, and let's go!" said David.

After retreating to safety, David called out to Saul and Abner. Rousing one another, they searched for the source of the voice. There on the ridge above their camp stood David and Abishai, Saul's spear and jug in hand, proof once again that David had been merciful and spared the king's life.

Stunned, the mighty warrior shook himself as though waking from a bad dream. Upon seeing David, his mind flashed back to the soothing melodies that had often allayed his madness, and the decade of faithful service in combat young David had given him.

The heart of King Saul sorrowed for sanity. He cried out despairingly to David, "I have sinned! Come back, David my son. I will not try to harm you again. I have been a fool!"

How David longed to be at peace with Saul and to return to his own people in Israel! How desperately he missed Jonathan! But, knowing all too well the changeable moods of the king's fever, he prepared to rejoin his band of outlaws.

Before descending on the other side of the hill, David called back to Saul in a clear, sober tone, "As surely as I valued your life today, so may the Lord value my life and deliver me from all trouble," and then walked away.

And Saul returned to Gibeah.

David's Pain

That night at David's camp, no one spoke to him. In the minds of his men, his mercy was inscrutable and the honor he gave the mad king, totally unnerving.

But since returning to camp, David was wrestling with his own doubts. What was to become of him after all? What future could he offer six hundred men whose patience was wearing thin?

It was one thing to avoid doing what was wrong, but quite another to proceed in doing what was right. Where, on earth, were they to go from here?

Tossing and turning on his bed that night, unable to slip into sleep, David cried out his lament to God.

O God, what is to become of me? I am forgotten by my people as though I were dead! I have become like broken pottery, useless and discarded, and there is terror on every side! His grief seemed to swallow him up as the night wore on and the darkness deepened.

Over and over he issued his lament, until the words at last ran together and exhaustion finally stilled his lips.

Sleep was brief and fitful that night.

Chapter Eleven

WHEN THE GREAT FALL

Abishai approached David early the next morning, while David was sitting alone outside his tent, lyre in hand but silent and songless. When he saw his friend coming, David lowered the lyre to his knee and waited silently for Abishai's greeting.

"David, may I speak with you?" the warrior and friend asked.

"Of course, Abishai. What is it?" David motioned for him to sit down on the large, flat rock beside him.

"Sir, you know that we're all grateful for the new lives you've given us," Abishai began, "and I swear any of us would gladly give his life for you," he added with conviction. Then he paused.

"But we need something else now. We need homes for our families—we want our children to grow up in one place, with real roofs over their heads.

"You understand, don't you, David?" Abishai pleaded, intently searching David's eyes. "Our wives are tired of moving continually, breaking and setting up camp over and over."

He saw David's expression soften, so he pressed on. "Doesn't Abigail feel the same way?"

The women these men have married along the way have indeed been patient, David mused to himself. Then his mind quickly went to Abigail, whom he had taken as his wife only months before, after she had been widowed at Carmel. (Michal had remained with Saul and remarried.)

"Yes, she feels the same way," David sighed. "This is no way to live."

Silence fell between them.

"Abishai, our friends are few. Nowhere among our people are we welcome as long as Saul lives." He ruefully added, "Perhaps the enemy of our enemy may be our best hope for a friend!" David turned and looked meaningfully into Abishai's eyes.

Silence again.

After a moment, "Do you mean the Philistines?" asked Abishai incredulously.

"Who else? We haven't personally fought them in years, and they well know our position with their greatest foe, Saul," David replied.

Then sighing and looking away from Abishai, David said wonderingly, "But what an unholy alliance that would be!"

A Strange Turn

The Philistines did indeed take them in. The city of Ziglag was even given them for their own, after a period of proving their loyalty as they lived and worked among the Philistines. Thus David, his men, and their families settled and grew, content to let the world go by.

So far removed did they feel from their true kinsmen in Israel, that when the Philistine army planned to move against Saul in battle once again, David and his men volunteered to march with them.

However, several days into the march, there arose suspicion among the highest commanders that, mid-battle, David might turn on them to regain Saul's favor, and so he and his men were sent home to Ziglag. In that decision, God moved on their behalf, protecting them from piercing their own brothers in battle.

But there was already a price to pay for briefly forgetting who they were—the seed of Abraham, Isaac and Jacob. During their brief absence, Ziglag had been raided and burned by the Amalekites, and their families had been taken captive!

How ironic, David thought to himself, *that the very people who had been spared by Saul years ago—against God's orders—have returned to plague his successor!*

What followed was but a blur to David: The men threatening to stone him, their mad pursuit of the raiding party, bloodshed, slaughter...and victory! But all the while, a Voice inside was insistently asking, "Who are you, David?"

As they marched home with their families alive and well, carrying plunder far beyond what had been stolen from Ziglag, David made a decision of spirit. After arriving, he sent gifts to all the elders of Judah who had befriended him in times past. He knew who he was again, and the deception was broken.

Foreboding Night

A few days later, while the Philistines were locked in combat with the armies of King Saul, David was awakened in the dead of night by an intense aching in his heart. Something grievous was happening! He could feel it!

David rose and, after throwing on a robe and sandals, stepped outside his house and looked up and down the street apprehensively.

Going to the western gate of the city, he climbed the stone steps to the top of the wall and scanned the desert sands in every direction.

A rumble of thunder broke in the distance, followed by a flash of lightning, and then more thunder. The air was stifling and still. More thunder to the west, only closer this time. Then a streak of lightning shot from the heavens straight down to the earth, and the wind began to blow!

Driven from his lookout post by the sand that was now filling the air—whipped by the gales coming from the western sky—David awkwardly descended the steps, clutching the stones of the wall to keep himself from being blown away!

As he groped through the storm back to his house, the pain in his heart intensified, causing him to call out:

"Saul! Saul!" The cry rose in agony from his heart, as his tears became mixed with the sand on his face. And David *knew*. The king had fallen!

Then as Jonathan's slain body came before him as though in a dream, David tore his robe and tunic and fell to the ground sobbing. "No, no, no!" he moaned.

"The great are no more! The king and his son are fallen! God help us all!" whispered David into the sand beneath his face, as the storm raged on.

Chapter Twelve

SHADOW OF THINGS TO COME

David's Mighty Men, now numbering in the thousands, awoke in the morning to the sad strains of David's lament for the slain Saul and Jonathan whom he had loved. Out of obedience to David they learned the melancholy dirge and sang it with their shepherd-warrior. Soon all of Judah seemed caught up in the sorrow of David's heart.

> *Your glory, O Israel,*
> *Lies slain on your heights.*
> *How the mighty have fallen!*
>
> *Saul and Jonathan—*
> *In life, loved and gracious,*
> *In death, never parted.*
>
> *Swifter than eagles,*
> *They were stronger than lions.*
> *How the mighty have fallen in battle!*
>
> *Daughters of Israel, weep for Saul;*
> *Jonathan, my brother, I grieve for you!*
> *How the mighty have fallen in battle!*[1]

David grieved deeply, refusing consolation even from those closest to him. Then on the third day, he inquired of God.

⤥ ──── ⤦

---

1   Adapted from 2 Samuel 1:19,23-26.

"What should I do, my Lord, now that Saul is no more and Your people lack a king?" he asked into the evening sky. "Show me the way to go and I will walk in it."

His mind went instantly back to the first night he spent in Saul's service after killing Goliath. He had gone up onto the roof of his small house to get some air, and below him had spread the sleeping city. "Our sheep have become the two-legged kind," he had murmured to God that night.

Are they now ready to be led? he wondered apprehensively.

And then, as surely as he lived, David began sensing the presence of God moving softly and gently about him, like a warm spring breeze promising a fruitful summer to come.

"It's time, son of Jesse. It's time!" a voice spoke clearly into his spirit.

He turned to look about for the source of the voice, but no one was there. A knowing look came into his eyes and he smiled just a little. The Lord was speaking to him as He had back in the days of sheepherding for his father!

"Go, David, to Mt. Hebron. It is time for Samuel's prophecy to be fulfilled, for there you will be crowned King of Judah!" came the solemn voice again. "They are waiting for you. I will bring the rest of Israel to you in due time." Then all was quiet.

David's heart started pounding, the weight of such a prospect settling upon his chest, making it almost hard to breathe!

But David went, hopes and dreams swirling about him as he traveled to Mt. Hebron.

He arrived a wandering son of promise and left, a shepherd-king of the tribe of Judah.

Struggle for Power

The ensuing seven and one-half years were filled with war as David struggled with the house of Saul for leadership of the remaining eleven tribes. As the years wore on, David's strength increased, while that of his adversaries weakened.

It seemed that all Israel had known about David's anointing by Samuel as a boy in Bethlehem. Whether conscripted into the Israelite army or serving with David in the desert, every man had heard of David's valor and faithfulness, and to all he was a hero. And as Saul's son Ish-Bosheth's power in Israel waned, mutiny was bound to come.

Then murder followed on its heels, unbeknown to David until the deeds were done. Ish-Bosheth and Abner, Saul's brave commander, were ruthlessly killed.

And David sorrowed again.

Unity at Last

Upon the deaths of their leaders, the rest of the tribes of Israel came to David at Mt. Hebron, begging him to be their king as well. Once more the anointing oil flowed down upon his head, running over his beard and onto the shoulders of the now-grown son of Jesse.

And then, as an elder of Israel lifted the crown high in the air for all to see, a hush swept the crowd before them. A moment after it descended upon the head of the kneeling David, a shout of victory exploded from the troops, followed by:

> "Long live the king!
> Praise to our God!
> Long live the king!"

Over and over rang the cheers of fealty to David and to their God. Such joy reigned! War was finally over between them, and they were standing before God's anointed as one man, together at last! Swords held high, armor gleaming in the sun, four hundred thousand soldiers marched in review before their newly-crowned king—their beloved David—shouting in cadence:

> "Long live the king!
> Praise to our God!
> Long live the king!"

And then as the men reassembled in ranks by tribe, stretching out in a semicircle before him, David dropped to his knees. He knew beyond a shadow of a doubt from where his authority to rule had come—not from people, but from a holy God, forever his Lord and King.

As a hush fell over the vast crowd, David unsheathed his sword and laid it upon the ground before him where he knelt. In a sacred moment of communion between this monarch and his God, David prayed.

> *O Lord, I rejoice in Your strength.*
> *How great is my joy in the victories You give!*
> *You have granted me the desire of my heart*
> *And have not withheld the request of my lips.*
>
> *You welcomed me with rich blessing*
> *And placed a crown of pure gold on my head.*
> *I asked You for life and You gave it to me—*
> *Length of days, for ever and ever.*
> *Through the victories You gave, my glory is great;*
> *You have bestowed on me splendor and majesty.*
> *Surely You have granted me eternal blessings*
> *And made me glad with the joy of Your presence.*
> *For I trust in the Lord;*
> *Through the unfailing love of the Most High*
> *I will not be shaken. Amen.*[2]

⌇ ———— ⌇

2   Adapted from Psalm 21:1-7.

David slowly rose to his feet, his eyes intently searching the faces of the gallant men before him. Satisfied with what he found in their eyes, he retrieved his sword from the ground and quickly strapped it again to his side. Then with both arms raised to the sky and his head thrown back, David let out a shout that resounded through the ranks that were at attention before him:

> *Be exalted, O Lord, in Your strength!*
> *We will sing and praise Your might!*[3]

This cry, like the last, was picked up and echoed by every man—four hundred thousand voices shouting praises to their God! The hills rang with the sounds of joy and the desert rejoiced that the Glory of Israel was to come to earth!

A profound sense of purpose and promise hung over Mt. Hebron and all who celebrated in the valley below. The seed of a great Kingdom had been sown this day—a Kingdom without end, whose power and glory King David could only imagine in his wildest dreams!

For the moment, what might unfold in the years to come—the joys and sorrows, the victories and betrayals, the sin and even the fulfilled promises—mattered little to the newly-crowned king of Israel. In the face of the vast unknown, to David it was enough to be bound to God at the heart.

Eyes of the Lamb

As he drifted off to sleep at the end of that long and glorious day, the eyes of the Lamb he had seen in the night sky some 21 years before came into focus in his dream. They curiously probed David's heart for a moment, then looked beyond

---

3   Psalm 21:13.

him into the distance, searching the sky for what, David did not know.

The king turned in his sleep, straining to see what it was that the Lamb sought in the inky blackness of the starless sky.

Then suddenly, in his dream, David found himself standing unnoticed in the street of a city that he had never seen before. It was a magnificent city, with towering minarets jutting into the azure sky at regular intervals along the outer walls, and palaces within. Crowds were gathering to the left just inside the city's main gate and the air was charged with festivity!

"He's coming! The King is coming!" Men, women with babes in their arms, and children all chattered at once while they rushed toward the crowd that was growing rapidly. As they ran, they were tearing palm branches from the trees and waving them wildly in the air!

"Hosanna to the King! Blessed is He who comes in the name of the Lord!" the shouts rang.

The Shepherd King

And then He appeared. Expecting to see the grandest monarch of all time being carried with pomp and circumstance through the gates, David's jaw dropped in amazement at what emerged as the crowd split to let the King through.

A plain man in a simple, nondescript robe gathered at the waist by a worn leather belt, rode astride a young donkey. His sandaled feet, dusty and calloused from endless miles of travel on foot, hung nearly to the ground from the sides of the small animal. His face and hands were bronzed from the sun, his hair and beard framed his features in soft brown tones.

As he neared the spot where David stood riveted to the ground, their eyes met for an instant. But in that instant, the "knowing" of a 12-year-old boy returned. The loving Shepherd-King of his vision long ago had left the heavens and had come to earth! This was He!

A New Purpose

David awoke with a start. He must find that city! He must prepare it for the Shepherd-King!

For a moment, he forgot the crossed beams and the specter of death upon them. Only the Eyes in the Night Sky gripped his heart, preventing thoughts of all else.

"Hosanna to the King! Blessed is He who comes in the name of the Lord!" rang in his ears as he bowed to the earth for his morning prayers.

Part II

HEART OF THE KING

Chapter Thirteen

THE MYSTICAL CITY

In the distance it stood, cool and aloof, the coveted prize of every nation that would ever seek to endure in this part of the world. Jerusalem—a jeweled fortress atop the formidable ridge of hills rising above the slender valleys—rested in the very heart of the land that God had given to the children of Israel.

It was a strange, haunting place, this desert giant, holding an allure for David that made his heart beat faster every time he glimpsed its towering walls. And when he was far from it, the ancient city called to him in his dreams. Promises of some far, distant future glory hung about the very word *Jerusalem*, as the young king savored it upon his tongue.

David had been fascinated by this city ever since he could remember, although he had never been inside its walls. Situated only a short distance north of his own hometown, Bethlehem, it was believed to have been Salem, the City of Peace, to where Abraham had taken tribute to Melchizedek, the very first priest and king of the living God! For David to establish his throne here would not only be politically and logistically wise, but also spiritually significant. But as David began his reign, it was the stronghold of the Jebusites. If the mystical city were to be his, it would have to be taken.

Good News

"Wait up!" Zachary excitedly called as he quickly dismounted his camel, dropping the reins in the sand. He ran to catch up with David, who was on his way to bathe in the stream behind the camp. "I've got great news!" he shouted.

David's face broke into a big smile as he turned to meet the young scout.

"Well, my friend. What did you find out for me on your trip to the 'mystical city'?" David probed, as he eagerly reached out to embrace Zachary in welcome, a towel and clean tunic hanging over his left shoulder. "Can we take it?"

"Well," Zachary began, after catching his breath and brushing the dust from his own tunic, "it's as I suspected—armed to the teeth. *But...*" at which he broke into a grin, "the aqueduct system carrying their water supply into the city from the Gihon Spring, although well-hidden, is undefended."

After a brief pause for effect, Zachary added in mock seriousness, "How well can you swim?"

"Hmmm...good question." David faked deep contemplation, dropping his head and furrowing his brow. Then looking up into Zachary's eyes he drolly responded, "About as well as you can, I daresay." At this, they both burst out laughing. Neither David nor his men had had much time to perfect the backstroke during their years in the desert!

"But we're fast learners, aren't we, my friend?" David asked with a chuckle.

"Yes, sir, we are!" shot back Zachary with great bravado.

David slipped easily into a command mode. "Then let's get ready. Make a map of the surrounding area and of every detail of the city you can remember. Get with Joab and begin planning our strategy for the offensive. Both of you, meet with me here at noon tomorrow." David grabbed Zachary's right hand and shook it, and then slapped him on the shoulder in congratulations.

Then seriously, "Jerusalem will be taken for our God, Zach, and I *know* that we're just the men to bring that to pass!" David said with a determined look in his eye and a set jaw.

Then his face softened as he dropped Zach's hand. "Our strength is in God, you know, my friend. By *His* might we will prevail!"

Zach turned back toward camp to find Joab, and David continued toward the stream, his heart dancing with excitement.

Victory

Jerusalem was indeed taken by David and his men. The strategy hinted at by the young scout, and then developed by the king and his commanders, worked flawlessly. By secretly entering the city through its aqueduct system, they subdued the Jebusites from within!

David was beside himself with joy! As he explored every inch of the regal city—its towering stone walls silent with dignity— it was as though he had "come home" to a kind of birthplace, even though he had never been here before.

Tears welled up in the young king's eyes. To himself he wondered, *Why am I so moved by every stone in this strange city?* Pausing for a moment, something of a revelation seemed to grip him. *Perhaps my heart knows something that my mind has yet to measure.* David shook his curly head and dried his eyes.

Clearing his throat and straightening his back, standing tall and dignified in the afternoon sun, David spoke aloud to the city itself, "You'll be my beloved home, the City of David and of our God! And more than that," he continued, beginning to raise his voice in passion and determination, "your very stones will forever shout to the world that there is a God in Heaven who hears and answers the cries of His people!"

Complications

As David settled into public life in Jerusalem, his private life became increasingly complex behind closed doors. In a culture where having multiple wives was the custom, David had taken two while in the desert and four more at Hebron, and was now demanding the return of Michal, the wife he had left behind when he had fled from Saul many years before.

"But, David," pleaded Abigail, "aren't we enough to keep you happy?"

"It's not that," he said softly, gently drawing her to his side on the couch in his sitting room. "It's just that she was wrongfully kept from me.

"Her father and brother are dead now, and I want to care for and protect her as I never could when we were first married and her father gave us no peace." David's gaze moved from Abigail's face to the window as he remembered.

"Did you know that she saved my life once when her father sent soldiers to kill me? She stalled them and covered for me while I made good my escape out the bedroom window." His voice dropped to a whisper as he turned to again look pleadingly into Abigail's eyes. "I never got to thank her. I never saw her again." Moved by the pain in David's eyes, Abigail reached over to comfort him, in spite of herself. Her touch startled David and brought him back to the present.

Regaining his composure he continued, matter-of-factly, "I have been told that Saul gave her to another in marriage to spite me. That marriage is nothing before God. She was my wife first! And I will have her back!"

Then gently again—more to himself than to Abigail—he added, "She loved me so. She will surely be glad to be with me again." At this, Abigail withdrew her hand from his shoulder and turned to look away.

David abruptly rose to go. "And so it is settled," he stated with finality. "It is right that she be restored to me."

Drawing Abigail to her feet and holding her soft, white face cupped in his hands, he added, "If you were stolen from me, I would move Heaven and earth to get you back!"

She sadly smiled and nodded. David kissed her and strode from the room. She closed the door slowly behind him and wept as she heard his footsteps fade into the distance.

Michal's Return

David's men went for Michal, but she did not return to him with the gratitude in her heart that he had anticipated. During the years he had been in exile and at war, she had given her heart to her new husband, and he his heart to her, and the parting was grievous. But David had not been there to see it.

However, the coldness of her affection in the nights ahead told him the story as surely as if he had torn her from the other man's arms himself.

A Dream Within a Vision

On one such night, David went walking alone about the streets of his "mystical" city, finding it easier to sort out his feelings under the stars just as he had as a shepherd boy.

As his steps led him toward the main gate of the city, David was suddenly stopped in his tracks, stunned by the uncanny familiarity of the scene before him. A puzzling conviction began to form in his heart. Sometime in the past, long before overtaking the city with his soldiers, he had stood right here in this street, at this very spot, facing the main gate! But how could that have been?

As King David strained to remember, he began to hear voices as well that he had heard before. They cried, "He's coming! The King is coming!"

And then it came back to him. He had seen and heard all this in his dream on the night of his coronation at Mt. Hebron! David stood transfixed by the reenactment of the dream—by the sights and sounds of the mystical surging crowd as they ran by him, tearing palm branches from the trees and waving them wildly in the air! "Hosanna! Blessed is He who comes in the name of the Lord!" rang the voices.

His eyes turned expectantly toward the massive gate, whose doors were now swung wide open. The King will surely appear!

That humble King in simple garb riding astride the donkey, just as David had seen Him in his dream before, should now come through the gate and proceed toward him along the dusty, palm-strewn street. Everything was the same. It was a vision containing his own dream!

But this time, before the King reached the place where David stood in the street, the scene slid out of focus and drifted away, the voices becoming muted and soon distant and indistinct.

How David hated to see the scene fade away! The young earthly king so longed to look into the tender eyes of the true King for whom he and his people had been waiting since the beginning of their history! For David was assured once again that the Shepherd-King of his dreams was He.

But now he understood his old and enduring fascination with this majestic city—why he had been so under compulsion to subdue and occupy it. David gasped as understanding flooded his mind. Someday the King of the crossed beams would come here, to this very city! He would enter the ancient gates that David now stood before in the middle of the night.

"Somehow I must prepare this city for the King's coming. My mission cannot be contained in mere rulership of a people, for I have seen the King!"

David rubbed his eyes, and then his head, for it ached with the intensity of his anticipation of the future reign of this heavenly monarch. How was this all to be?

There in the darkness, peace flooded the heart of Israel's new king, and a song poured from his mouth to his God:

How dearly have You loved Your servant,
How gladly will I praise You among the people!

By day You tune my ear to Your voice
And You counsel me in the night.

Hide me in the shadow of Your wings.
Hear my cry and grant me courage, O my God!

And I, in righteousness will see Your face!
O Lord my God, the King of kings.[1]

That night David dreamed of angels in the sky.

---

1   Adapted from various Psalms.

Chapter Fourteen

THE HOMECOMING

The complexion of the city was changing quickly under the direction of the poet king. The city fairly shone in the morning sunlight. The stones of the aged towers and minarets were sanded until they looked as though they had just been quarried, and the weathered city gates—gleaming with fresh polish—opened silently and majestically on well-oiled hinges. The streets were brushed clean, the walls of all the homes were patched and scrubbed and flowers bloomed everywhere.

As an act of peace and friendship, Cyrus, King of Tyre, sent his own carpenters, craftsmen, and artisans—along with all the cedar timbers and building materials that would be needed—to construct a palace for King David. While the Israelites in Jerusalem were busy refurbishing their city, King Cyrus' men were building a palace more beautiful than David ever could have imagined!

David consulted God on every decision and, as a result, wherever he turned his hand of leadership, enemies were subdued and more riches poured into the kingdom. Prosperity and peace were coming to Israel at last.

The King's Plan

Several months later, two men stood on the rooftop of the nearly-finished palace at midday. One wore the spartan garb of prophet and holy man, while the other was robed in a fine linen tunic edged with gold and purple stitching. Looking southward, they surveyed the entire city—all nine acres of it. Jerusalem was perched atop the southernmost of three hills that comprised the impressive ridge that rose straight up out of the desert, with deep valleys on either side.

Behind the men to the north were the other two hills—the nearer of which was Mt. Moriah, where Abraham had taken Isaac to be sacrificed centuries before, now owned by Araunah the Jebusite.

Nathan and David were deeply engaged in conversation.

"It could go right there, David," said Nathan in his gravelly voice, pointing to the courtyard easily visible to them from their rooftop vantage point. "What do you think?" he queried the king, as he stroked his graying beard.

David nodded his head vigorously in agreement. "Exactly what I was thinking. From there it would be accessible to everyone within our walls and equally well-protected from any gate of the city," he said with satisfaction.

"First thing tomorrow," David continued, "I will select workmen for the task of clearing the area and erecting a tent to house and protect the Ark after we bring it here from Obed-Edom's home. It'll be a tight fit, for there is little extra space in this crowded city," laughed David, "but I think we can fit it in with enough room left for a courtyard for the altar."

A moment of silence passed between the men as David shifted his gaze from the scene below to the sky above. He watched with curiosity as a cloud shaped much like an eagle formed in the vast blue expanse over their heads. Then, with a tinge of sadness the king exclaimed, "How I wish Samuel were still alive to celebrate with us when the Ark of God comes to Jerusalem! How I miss him!" he sighed wistfully as the eagle-shaped cloud slid out of focus and was blown away.

After a brief pause, the king's thoughts returned to the Ark. "I have heard how wonderfully God has blessed Obed-Edom and his household since the Ark has been in his care," he quietly reflected, then added quickly, "but that is not why I want it here. God's blessing has followed me all the days of my life and I need not covet it."

Cocking his head to one side and eyeing Nathan thoughtfully, David said matter-of-factly, "Obedience and devotion are the stuff of blessing, Nathan. Don't you think so?" he asked, but then continued without waiting for an answer. "And visions from God are important, aren't they?"

Nathan returned David's thoughtful look knowingly, without saying a word. None was needed. David longed to tell Nathan about his visions and dreams, but now was not the time.

With passion David went on, "How I long to worship Him and to encourage Israel to return to Him with all their hearts! My friend, can you imagine?" the king's eyes glistened with excitement as he pointed to the courtyard in the distance. "The very Ark of the Covenant that went before our people in the wilderness—the dwelling place of God's Presence during those years of miracles and deliverance—will be right here in Jerusalem! Each and every day we will be able to come into His presence in worship as they did long ago!" His voice fairly exploded with his delight at the prospect.

Then David's tone quieted and softened, without losing a bit of its intensity. He ran his tanned fingers through his curly hair as he looked into the distance.

With a faraway look in his eyes, he continued. "All the grandeur, all the suffering, all the holiness, all the mystery and promise of our calling is wrapped up in the Ark. It is our talisman, Nathan, our heartbeat, our soul, until the Messiah comes."

It was Nathan's turn then to show emotion. As he laid his hand tenderly upon David's shoulder, tears rolled down his leathery cheeks and dropped silently onto his rough tunic. In that intense moment, Nathan had no words.

The two men embraced there on the rooftop, then Nathan turned to go, carefully descending the steep stairway from the roof to the ground.

David stayed behind to pray. As he knelt down on the simple reed mat that he had laid upon the dusty floor, his words came out earnestly, in little more than a whisper to his God. Humbly he prayed:

One thing I ask of You, Lord,
This is what I seek

That I may dwell
In Your house
All the days of my life,

To gaze upon Your beauty,
O my Lord
And to seek You in Your temple.

For in the day of trouble
You will keep me safe
In Your dwelling;

You will hide me in the shelter
Of Your tabernacle
And set me high upon a rock.

At Your tabernacle will I sacrifice
With shouts of joy;
I will sing and make music to You, Lord.[1]

1   Adapted from Psalm 27:4-6.

I would rather be a doorkeeper
In the house of my God
Than dwell in the tents of the wicked.

For You, O Lord,
Are a sun and shield;
You bestow favor and honor.

No good thing do You withhold
From those
Whose walk is blameless.

How blessed is the man
Who trusts in You!
Amen.[2]

As he rose from prayer, an unbidden question pressed in upon him.

"What price is this earthly king willing to pay to see true worship of the heavenly King come to earth?" he heard himself ask aloud. Immediately the lamb that he had seen on the family altar in his youth took form before him. Its eyes probed his, then closed in death! David held his breath at the sight, as his own question returned to pierce his heart.

"God, help me!" David cried. "Search me and teach me! Prepare me!"

After a moment of silent waiting on God, David peered down again upon the future site of the Ark. A bittersweet song played softly in his spirit.

⸎ ────── ⸎

2   Adapted from Psalm 84:10b-12.

85

The Ark Comes

The day the Ark was carried into Jerusalem by the Levites, with every tribe marching in rank behind them, cries of jubilation and high praise echoed among the hills and played across the plains for miles and miles around. David, throwing aside his royal robes and wearing only a simple garment of worship, danced before the Lord with all his might amid the sound of trumpets, tambourines, cymbals, and shouts of joy. It was the happiest day of his life!

⌐ Chapter Fifteen ⌐

THE PROPHECY

David awoke with a start. What was that noise? The sounds of hammers, chisels, and the grinding of blocks of stone being shaped to fit tightly against one another shattered the morning stillness.

How could this be? David wondered to himself as he rubbed the sleep from his eyes. *The Ark is securely in place and this palace was finished long ago. No new building should be going on!*

He grabbed his robe, stepped into sandals, splashed water into his face from the basin on his nightstand and headed for the stairway to the lookout tower located on the roof of his palace. The sounds were coming from within the city, but voices could be heard calling from the direction of Mt. Moriah, the barren hilltop beyond the northern limits of Jerusalem!

As he ascended the stairway, the noise grew louder and more definite—that of construction, the shouting of orders and measurements from one workman to another. But when he reached the pinnacle of the tower and looked toward Mt. Moriah, the sounds ceased as mysteriously and suddenly as they had begun! Except for the crowing of a few early-rising roosters below him down in the city streets, all was quiet.

But as he fixed his eyes to the north, there before him was not a barren hilltop boasting only clumps of dry thicket, but rather the most beautiful temple he had ever seen! Silent and holy it stood there, towering over the neighboring hills and looking down upon the deep natural valleys to the east and to the west as though they were its subjects. Alone and majestic, glittering in the morning sun, it seemed to have come down from the sky—from Heaven itself! How could mere man have ever imagined, much less built, such a grand house even for Jehovah!

Glancing back over his shoulder and down upon Jerusalem, the temporary tented tabernacle seemed absurd in comparison. Why, even his own cedar palace was far grander than what he had provided for God!

Eagerly turning back to study once again the temple on its holy hill, David couldn't believe his eyes! Now it was gone!

"Watchman," he called to the guard on the nearby wall. "By any chance did you see a temple out there on Mt. Moriah a few minutes ago?"

The guard looked at the king a bit strangely and then answered respectfully, "No, sir, I don't believe I did."

"Of course not," David uncomfortably replied. "Obviously there's nothing there." He cleared his throat and began humming a melody to cover up for what seemed a ridiculous question.

"It must have been a dream," David said to himself, "seen only with the eyes of my spirit. I know it was there."

As he stood gazing in the direction of the imaginary temple, he could remember exactly how it looked and roughly what its dimensions were, and clearly grasped how it should be constructed. Then he dashed back down the long stairway to his quarters and asked one of his servants to bring a scribe to his chambers right away. Meanwhile, he dressed and rehearsed the details of the temple so that he wouldn't forget them.

When Zephaniah the scribe arrived, David was more than ready for him. Forgetting food and his previous plans for the day, David secluded himself with the scribe, focusing only upon making sure that all the dimensions of the temple and its rooms, as well as descriptions of articles of worship that should be in them, were recorded accurately.

Sunset was approaching by the time they neared the end of the task. After checking everything carefully, David dismissed Zephaniah. Rising slowly from his chair, he straightened his tired back and stepped away from the desk for the first time that day.

He sought the rooftop again, reaching it just as the red-orange, glowing orb of the sun began dipping below the rim of the desert sand to the west. Never had he seen such a brilliant sunset!

His eyes hungrily sought the outline of Mt. Moriah in the twilight. Blue-gray shadows played across her rocky ridges and deepened the mystery that clung to her crown.

In his imagination, David could see the temple resting right where Abraham and Isaac had once stood in surrender to their God. Near the front gate of the magnificent structure was a thicket like that which had given up its prey for Isaac's sake—the ram that then died in his place.

"And then through Isaac's life came mine!" David marveled. "And through mine will come the final sacrifice as surely as God lives!"

Stunned by the very words he had just uttered, David raised his arms skyward, his heart filled with wonder.

On the Rooftop Again

David called for Nathan early the next morning. They met once again on the rooftop of the palace. He slowly and carefully shared the vision with Nathan, watching him for any signs of disbelief or ridicule. He saw none. Nathan became as excited as David had been the day before!

"Build it, David!" Nathan encouraged. "Build it just as soon as you see fit! God is with you, my son! It will be done!"

David slept little that night. He could think of nothing but the temple he intended to build.

Nathan slept little that night as well, but for a different reason. The prophet was being given a message from God for David that he had mixed feelings about delivering.

Nathan sought the king's presence the following morning in his throne room.

"Nathan, come in!" called David when he saw him at the door. Looking at him curiously, he asked, "So, what is on your mind that you seek me so urgently? More news about the temple I will build?" David couldn't suppress a happy grin.

"Well, yes and no." The prophet hesitated a moment, then pressed on.

"David, I was wrong when I encouraged you to build," he said apologetically. "I should have asked God first." At this, David's face fell, the grin fading quickly from his lips. "But I have a further message for you from the Lord, a very serious and wonderful one," he added encouragingly.

David regained his composure and beckoned Nathan to sit down in the chair beside him. "Please go on, Nathan. What God says is more important than any plan or dream I will ever have, no matter how dear it may be to me. Please tell me what He has told you."

So Nathan began. "Here is the message. God said that He has never been discontent with the simple Tabernacle that now rests in Jerusalem's courtyard. Through all the years of wandering with the children of Israel in the wilderness and the years of temporary sites since then, He never asked for more than what He was given."

The prophet chose his words carefully and spoke gently to his dear king. "He knows your heart, David, and the purity of your desire, but you will not be the one to build the Temple. It will be your son instead. After you die, it will be done."

After the disappointing news fully registered on David, the king asked anxiously, "But it will be done, truly, Nathan?" At Nathan's affirmative nod, David sighed in relief. "I'm glad." Then sensing that the prophet had more to say, David motioned to him to continue.

"David, He said to tell you that He took you from the pasture and from following the flock to be ruler over His people. He has been with you constantly and has cut off all your enemies."

Then as if making a pronouncement that could shake the world, Nathan declared solemnly, "He will now make your name like the name of the greatest men of the earth, David. He will also provide a place for His people Israel and will give them a home of their own, no more to be disturbed. In that day they will be oppressed no longer as they have been in the past!" Nathan's eyes filled with tears but he pressed on.

"And for this son of yours who will build the Temple, God Himself will establish his kingdom forever. He will be a father to him, and he a son to God. The Lord promises never to take His love away from him as He did Saul, and He will discipline him when he needs it."

After pausing for effect, Nathan declared with significance, "Out of you, David, will come a kingdom that will last forever!" Then dropping to his knees before the throne, Nathan quietly began to lift his praises to the Lord God for His Word and His faithfulness to His people.

David sat there, dumbfounded, as the divine pronouncement began to sink in. After several minutes both men rose to their feet, embraced, and then parted in silence.

Before the Lord

After Nathan's departure, the king hurried to the Tent and went in to sit before the Lord.

At first he didn't know what to say, but then slowly and humbly the words began to come. He prayed, "O Sovereign

Lord, who am I and what is my family that You have brought me this far? And now You speak of the future as well! How can this be? What more can I say to You? You know me, O Lord. For the sake of Your Word and according to Your will, You have done this great thing and made it known to Your servant."

With awe and gratitude David continued pouring his heart out to the Lord he so deeply loved. "How great You are, O Sovereign Lord! There is no one like You! And who is like Your people Israel, the one people You went out to redeem for Yourself, to make a name for You as You perform wonders before the nations? You have established Your people Israel as Your very own forever, and You, O Lord, have become their God!" On his face before the Lord, David worshiped and praised his God.

Rising to his knees, his hands raised toward Heaven, David spoke again. "And now, Lord God, keep forever the promise You have made about Your servant and his house. Do as You have promised so that Your name will be great forever. The men of this world will say, *'The Lord Almighty is God over Israel!'* and Your servant's house will be established forever."

Spontaneous adoration welled up within the worshiping king of Israel. "O Sovereign Lord, You are God! Your words are trustworthy, and You have promised these good things to Your servant. Now be pleased to bless the house of Your servant, that it may continue forever in Your sight, for You have spoken. With Your blessing my house will be blessed forever."[1]

When he finally rose to go, his knees were weak and wobbly beneath him. As he had seen the glory of God, he had also seen his own frailty.

---

1   Drawn from David's prayer in First Chronicles 17.

"Who am I to bear such blessing? O God, be my strength! Guide me. Destroy my weakness and foolishness! Teach me Your ways or I will perish!"

David slowly returned to his throne room. He had never felt weaker, but never more sure of his destiny.

~ Chapter Sixteen ~

MIGHTY WARRIOR

The Lord gave David victory wherever he went. Over time, he defeated the Philistines and the Moabites, ancient enemies of Israel. He also subdued the king of Zobah and the Arameans of Damascus, taking great plunder from them and making them subject to him.

When his men struck down 18 thousand Edomites in the Valley of Salt, David's name became great and feared among all the nations. Those not yet defeated by this dauntless king sought peace with him, offering to pay him tribute. David's name was perhaps the greatest in all the earth at that time in history.

All this warfare kept David away from home a great deal of the time. He returned periodically only to deliver gold and silver articles taken in battle, which would be dedicated to the Lord—and wives whom he had gained in treaties with other nations. It was the way of the world at that time.

The way of the world was also to claim credit for one's own victories. This David did not indulge in, although slowly but surely he was beginning to think he could do no wrong. He was to discover that success can expose a man's weakness more surely than failure.

With the wives came divided loyalty. With competition of affection came—strangely enough—isolation. Deep intimacy of heart and soul could not be shared with so many. And with so many, could not the preciousness of a single life be lost?

The Lure of Ease

David still sang and played the lyre for his troops as he had while on the run from King Saul years before. Every man but the hardest of heart was deeply moved by David's haunting melodies of devotion to His God. But beyond being an inspiration to his men, he was also the envy—however kindly—of many of them.

"Does anything ever go wrong for you, my king?" one young soldier asked wonderingly after dinner one night in the desert.

David laughed softly. "These days, you wouldn't think so, would you, Zeb? But it wasn't always this way, you know." David tossed another branch into the campfire. "But I guess the hard times are behind me now." David broke into a big grin. "Life couldn't be better! God's blessings have been tremendous!"

The boy just nodded in vigorous agreement and continued to look admiringly at his king. At that moment his commander Joab joined them, just in time to catch David's next comment.

"But I'm getting a little weary of all this fighting!" he continued with a laugh and a slap to Zeb's knee, as he leaned toward the boy.

Then dropping the jocularity, David grew serious. "I think I've done enough for awhile. I'd like to stay home from the next campaign and see what life in the city is like." Glancing at Joab who was now seated to his right he asked, "What do you think of that?"

Furrows began to form in Joab's brow. "I'm not sure I agree with the idea. Sure, we can do the fighting without you. But you are our commander. Your duty is to us, if you will pardon my bluntness. Just one more campaign and we can all stay home for awhile."

At this remark, everyone within earshot cheered!

"I'll consider your advice, Joab. But doesn't a king get to relax once in awhile and enjoy his wives?" His pleading smile as usual disarmed Joab.

"Do as you wish and stay home!" he laughed. "But with so many wives to make happy, where will you begin?" At this everyone laughed.

As David drifted off to sleep that night, his thoughts were not on temples, Lambs or Shepherd-Kings, but on the soft warmth of yet another unknown conquest—the one that might before long fill his arms.

The Trap

And so, in the spring, at the time when kings go off to war, David sent Joab out with the king's men and the whole Israelite army. They destroyed the Ammonites and began the siege of Rebbah. But David remained in Jerusalem.

On one particularly warm evening soon after Joab and the army had left on the campaign, David sought his rooftop for cooler air. In addition to being hot and sticky, he was bored and not a bit tired. He hadn't expected relaxing at home to be so tedious!

As he idly paced off the perimeter of his palace from his commanding post high above the city, his eye caught the glimmer of moonlight being reflected in a pool of water. There appeared to be a bath nestled among hanging plants on the roof of a small home a short distance away. By the way in which the moonlight rippled upon the surface of the water, someone must be seeking fresh air and relief from the heat in its cool waters. *My, how refreshing such a bath would be right now*, he thought.

There was not another movement in the city. It seemed as though only he and this night bather existed in the silvery moonlight. He remained transfixed by the shimmering movement on that garden rooftop.

Then, slowly, a graceful woman's form rose from the bath—lovely, white as alabaster, enchanting as a poet's tale! Her long, dark hair fell in waves upon her shoulders. He could not see her face distinctly at this distance, but he had seen enough to be enticed by this "goddess" in the night. He watched, spellbound, as she leisurely dried herself with a voluminous towel and then slipped into a filmy nightgown.

He must meet her! David climbed the steps to the lookout on the northern rim of the palace roof and addressed the guard who was watching the terrain toward Mt. Moriah.

"Beautiful night, isn't it, Eliel?"

"Yes, Your Majesty," Eliel answered, a bit surprised to see that his visitor was the king himself.

"Look back over this way, Eliel. Do you see the rooftop with the bath—the one with the lady walking about on it?" David casually asked, trying not to seem overly anxious for information.

The watchman looked where David was pointing, and after seeing the woman, turned back questioningly to David.

"Who is she, Eliel? Do you know?"

"Why, I believe that is Uriah's house. So it must be Bathsheba, his wife, my king," he replied simply.

"Ah, so it must be," agreed David. "Thank you, Eliel." He turned to go. "Good night, Eliel."

"Good night, sir."

Heart pounding, David tried to keep an unhurried pace as he crossed the roof from the foot of the tower to the stairway leading to his quarters below. Once upon the stairs, he nearly fell in his haste to reach the bottom! He then summoned the palace courier from his sleep and sent him with a message to Bathsheba.

"Go at once and bring her to me," ordered David, trying to make it sound like a normal request. "I know it's the middle of the night, but that's all right. She is awake. And, uh, you needn't awaken anyone else. Just go quickly and quietly. That's a good lad." David's palms were sweaty as he patted the courier on the back to hurry him along.

Will she come? David wondered as he paced back and forth in his chambers, waiting for her arrival. "Of course, she will," David said aloud as he smoothed out the curls in his hair with a comb and held a cool, wet cloth against his hot face. "I'm the King of Israel!" he added confidently.

"What I ask is a small thing," he reasoned. "Shouldn't such beauty be commended personally when it is so great? She deserves to be praised by a king!" assuring himself of the innocence of his midnight request. "But why is there this foreboding in my spirit?" The question pricked at his mind for but a moment, then he pushed it aside.

"I am her king and she, the wife of an old friend. What harm can come of this meeting? What harm, indeed?"

He quickly finished freshening himself in preparation for her coming.

And the trap was set.

Chapter Seventeen

STOLEN LOVE

The beautiful Bathsheba came. Perhaps she had loved him from a distance for years; perhaps not. But once she was within his reach behind closed doors, quiet conversation moved to passion within the space of a single touch.

Bathsheba slipped away from the palace as the sun's ray began stealing through the tall, half-shuttered windows of the royal bed chamber. David started in his sleep.

Alone With His Sin

During the days ahead, David busied himself with palace duties and the just governing of a nation. But at night his sin replayed before his eyes, now without ecstasy—only horror.

How he wished he had gone with his men! What a fool he had been! The poet-king's lyre lay still and no music stirred his heart at any time, day or night. His spirit was desolate.

And the torture continued. "My God, what have I done?" David cried out as he sought the Lord day after day.

But all was silent. The worst had arrived—God would not speak to him. He was alone with his sin.

Worship became a futile and painful experience. As he knelt and tried to pray, the image of the seventh commandment—written by the finger of God on the stone tablets concealed in the Ark, which he loved—burned into his soul relentlessly.

Each day he tried to persuade himself that no one would know of nor care about his affair that night. The courier seemed to have forgotten his midnight mission, and the watch-man never again mentioned David's inquiry after her that night. He seemed to be in the clear.

But try as he might, he could not seem to breathe freely anymore. The air always seemed clotted around him. He was never refreshed—his heart thundering within him at each recurring memory of that night.

And then the word he had feared most came from Bathsheba: She was pregnant...with his child. Uriah was away and there had been no one else near her. Panic grew in the king's heart hour by hour.

What am I to do? David broke into a sweat as he paced back and forth before the throne. The massive columns and ornately carved cedar walls seemed to shrink into common-ness as his mind searched the world's philosophies for an answer.

Abruptly he stopped pacing, a glimmer of frantic hope springing into his eyes. *I'll dispatch word to Joab to send Uriah home! He will lie with his wife and all will be well! When she bears the child, he can simply believe that it is his!*

After applauding himself for his brilliance, he strode from the room and issued the orders for Uriah's return.

Increasing Torture

But it was not to be so easy. Uriah was a greater man than David in the arena of faithfulness to his comrades-in-arms.

Uriah had been with David from the beginning—one of David's own Mighty Men, one of the original 37 of his closest and most valiant friends in the desert—back when no throne seemed likely. And he was still a soldier through and through; while others were bearing hardship on the field, he would do no less, even if confined to the city. To lie with his wife while they slept in tents was unthinkable! He spent the night with the servants, sleeping on a mat outside the door of the palace.

No matter what the king did to try to weaken his resolve, Uriah would not sleep with his wife. His loyalty to his calling and duty was unnerving—and exasperating—to David. Finally Uriah was returned to the field—without having cooperated in the least with David's deceptive scheme.

The pain in David's heart intensified. Each morning he arose from another sleepless night exhausted, driven only by the adrenaline of the fear of exposure. It seemed that his very bones ached from the pressure of his guilt. God's presence, when he felt it, was not a comfort but a hand heavy with conviction. Never had he felt such torture!

And the torture was to increase, for even greater evil yet lurked in the recesses of David's soul. This king who had danced before the Ark, this man after God's own heart who had hungered only for His Presence in the days of old, this same David ordered Joab to set Uriah up to be killed in battle!

Thus Uriah, his noble and faithful friend and fellow warrior, was placed on the front line under massive fire and then deserted by his own troops—at the command of the king—who murdered him as surely as if he had run Uriah through with his own royal blade!

After allowing Bathsheba a time of mourning for Uriah, David called for her and they were married. As they lay together after the wedding, there was silence between them. Sorrow and regret played in the shadows of the royal bridal chamber—twin specters that kept them both awake.

King David tossed restlessly. Bathsheba stared numbly at the patterns on the wall.

Haunting Guilt

They never talked about it with each other; it was too painful. But the pain drove them together as they waited for the child to be born. In a strange way, they both hoped that this new little life would wash away the past and bring joy to the palace once more.

David began making plans for this child. If it was a boy, he would see to it that this son would some day sit on the throne. If a girl, she would be a beauty like her mother and a delight to everyone at court. Whichever it was and whatever the plan, at the child's birth, music would return to David's heart, he was certain! And the smile would play about Bathsheba's precious face once again, driving away forever the look of worry and sadness that had held captive her spirit since Uriah's death.

"Is it my fault, David, that Uriah died in battle?" asked Bathsheba suddenly one evening after gazing pensively out of the bedroom window for what seemed a very long time to David. "Did God take his life to punish me for my unfaithfulness?" Her voice had dropped to a whisper.

The questions hit him hard. He stopped writing at his desk, drew a deep breath, and then went quickly to her side at the window.

"Shh! Don't even think such a thing." David drew her onto his lap. "You did nothing but obey the king, just as Uriah was obeying by defending his nation in battle," he earnestly assured her.

And then, turning his face toward the window so she couldn't read his heart through his eyes, he added calmly, "And soldiers sometimes die. It can't be helped when arrows fly and swords clash, now can it?"

She laid her head on his shoulder and heaved a sigh. They remained there together at the window until the evening shadows spread their long fingers across the city below and began their way up the palace wall.

A knock at the door made them both jump. "May I enter and light the evening lamps?" the voice of a servant called softly.

The Pain Deepens

After Bathsheba was asleep that night, David sought the window again, his heart aching. All was dark below, except in the towers along the ancient wall where lamps burned dimly, keeping the watchmen company at their lonely posts.

"O God, I have become like a man who does not hear, whose mouth can offer no true reply," he whispered into the night. As the tears rolled down his cheeks he continued his one-sided dialogue with his God who had been silent all these many months.

"O Lord, do not forsake me! Be not far from me, O my God!" he whispered as he wept.

Chapter Eighteen

THE PROPHET'S STORY

David had convinced himself that no one would ever know what he had done. But everyone did. From the servants in the kitchen, to the soldiers on the field, to the kings of rival nations—everyone knew. Gossip flew among the people of Israel and across the boundary lines of kingdoms. The shepherd-king—whose sheer innocence and devotion to God had once caused multitudes to fall before Jehovah—was the laughingstock of dignitaries far and wide and the painful disappointment of his subjects.

The king had become so self-deceived, he went on as though nothing at all had happened! But his ability to see into the hearts of his people had vanished; his sins had closed his spiritual eyes till he could see only what he wanted to see. However, as he yearned for the return of God's favor, God birthed a plan for resolution.

Day of Reckoning

The sin must be dealt with, or his fellowship with God would never be restored nor his vision returned. So God gave Nathan, David's dearly-loved advisor and Israel's prophetic voice, a story to tell David—one that would strip the blindness from his eyes and the chains from his heart.

When Nathan sought an audience with the king, he was quickly ushered into the throne room. Seeing the grim look on Nathan's face, the furrows in his forehead, and the droop of his shoulders, David quickly dismissed the guards and servants until the two of them were standing face to face, alone. They embraced briefly, then eyed one another carefully.

"David, please sit down," Nathan began wearily. "I want you to listen with your heart to the story I have to tell you."

Puzzled, David obediently sat down upon his throne. After a moment of silence, Nathan cleared his throat and began in low, even tones to tell the tale, watching David as he spoke.

The Story

"There were two men in a certain town, one rich and the other poor. The rich man had a very large number of sheep and cattle, but the poor man had nothing except one little ewe lamb he had bought. He raised it, and it grew up with him and his children. It shared his food, drank from his cup, and even slept in his arms. It was like a daughter to him." David was listening intently, so Nathan continued telling the story just as God had told it to him.

"Now a traveler came to the rich man, but the rich man refrained from taking one of his own sheep or cattle to prepare a meal for the traveler who had come to him. Instead, he took the ewe lamb that belonged to the poor man and prepared it for the one who had come to him."

At this, David burned with anger against the man and, forgetting himself, shouted, "That's outrageous! As surely as the Lord lives, the man who did this deserves to die! He must pay for that lamb four times over, because he did such a thing and had no pity." The king was livid.

Looking David hard in the eyes, Nathan said firmly, "*You* are the man!" In shock, David sat riveted to his seat. Nathan continued, sparing nothing.

"This is what the Lord, the God of Israel, says: 'I anointed you king over Israel, and I delivered you from the hand of

Saul. I gave everything your master had to you. I also gave you the house of Israel and Judah. And if all this had been too little, I would have given you even more. Why did you despise the word of the Lord by doing what is evil in His eyes?' " The prophet's eyes burned into David as he continued.

" 'You struck down Uriah the Hittite with the sword and took his wife to be your own. You killed him with the sword of the Ammonites. Now, therefore, the sword will never depart from your house, because you despised me and took the wife of Uriah the Hittite to be your own.' "

David cried out and then fell back in his chair. While he had been nagged by guilt before, he was now devastated by the full-blown revelation of the depth of his wickedness before God!

Nathan was not finished. "This is what the Lord says: 'Out of your own household I am going to bring calamity upon you. Before your very eyes I will take your wives and give them to one who is close to you, and he will lie with them in broad daylight! You did it in secret, but I will do this thing in broad daylight before all Israel.' "

Then David cried out in despair, "I have sinned against the Lord, Nathan! I thought before that it was merely against Uriah, but now I see the horror of it in God's eyes! Nathan, what will become of me? I deserve to die!" David's words ended in an agonized whisper.

Putting his hands gently on David's heaving shoulders, Nathan replied more gently, "The Lord has taken away your sin, David. You are not going to die. But because by doing this you have made the enemies of the Lord show utter contempt, the son born to you will die." Stunned by Nathan's words, David silently buried his face in his hands, his body slumping forward until his elbows rested on his knees.

Nathan turned and quietly left the room, shaking his head to the staff not to disturb the king until he called for them.

David's Plea

After Nathan had gone home, the child whom Bathsheba had borne to David became ill. In tears, David pleaded with God to spare the child.

For six days David mourned and fasted, spending the nights lying on the ground rather than in his bed. How he begged God for the life of his son!

"David, get up from the ground! And eat something, please!" the elders of the royal household implored the king. "You must go on. You must keep your strength in order to rule!" But he would listen to no one. As long as the child was alive, he had hope that perhaps God would relent.

Bathsheba's Sorrow

Alone with the dying child, Bathsheba wept and held him close. By this time she had pieced together the story of how Uriah had died, and she was overwhelmed by grief at the prospect of losing now even this remaining tiny part of her life.

And a further fear gripped her. "If the child dies, will David desert me?" she wondered aloud to herself. "Did he marry me only to cover his sin? Was it not for love at all?" These questions beat upon her mind as she feverishly nursed the child who, despite her efforts, became weaker and weaker each day.

On the seventh day her son died.

When David heard the news, he quietly arose and bathed and ate. The issue was settled. God had done as He had said and there was no reason to plead further. He went before the Lord to make peace at last. Alone on his knees he prayed:

Have mercy on me, O God,
According to Your unfailing love;
According to Your great compassion
Blot out my transgressions!

Wash away all my iniquity
And cleanse me from my sin.
Against You, You only, have I sinned
And done what is evil in Your sight.

Cleanse me with hyssop,
And I will be clean;
Wash me, and I will be whiter than snow.
Let the bones You have crushed rejoice.

Do not cast me from Your presence
Or take Your Holy Spirit from me!
Restore to me the joy of Your salvation
And grant me a willing spirit, to sustain me.

You do not delight in sacrifice,
Or I would bring it;
The sacrifices of God are a broken spirit;
A broken and contrite heart You will not despise.[1]

"O God, how great is Your mercy! How wonderful Your forgiveness! Before You and You alone will I bow in worship all the days of my life," prayed the broken king of Israel.

1   Adapted from Psalm 51.

The King's Response

David did not cast Bathsheba aside as she had feared. As the peace of God, which had been absent for these many months, again flooded his soul, David longed to comfort her.

He knocked gently at her door. He could hear her weeping within, and his heart was pierced afresh by the sorrow that his sin had brought upon his household. For a moment he was tempted to avoid facing her. He turned to retreat back down the hall. But the peace of God had come to stay, and from it he drew courage.

He knocked again, more loudly this time. Her handmaiden opened the door hesitantly, then at his urging, stepped back to allow him to enter. David gently motioned for her to go to her chambers and leave them alone. She bowed and obeyed, closing the door quietly behind her.

Bathsheba was sitting in her favorite chair facing the window, sobbing. When she heard him enter, she turned in expectation of the worst.

But David simply knelt beside her, reaching to take her hands in his.

In broken tones he asked sadly, "Can you forgive me, Bathsheba?" Without waiting for her reply, he gravely continued, "In my selfishness I have stolen everything from you! I do not deserve your love or your company."

He paused, searching her face for signs of forgiveness. After a moment he continued, "God has amazingly forgiven me! Will you start over again with me as well?"

Stroking her arm tenderly, he added, "You have had to share my punishment, and I am so sorry! My only consolation is that we will see our son again—in Heaven. God has spoken to my heart that he is there, even now!" Joy flashed briefly over her countenance, and then grief returned.

"Please forgive me," he begged. "Dear Bathsheba, I do love you so!" he whispered as he sought her eyes with his.

"Oh, David, is there hope for us?" she asked sadly.

He gathered her into his arms, gently wiping her tearstained cheeks with the back of his hand.

That night the specters of guilt that had dogged their nights in the past were gone, and sleep was sweet. While Bathsheba dreamed of sunshine and laughing children, David dreamed of the Lamb and the mercy of the King.

New Hope

Exactly nine months later, another son was born. On the morning of Solomon's birth, a promise was secretly whispered by David into Bathsheba's ear...

Chapter Nineteen

BETWEEN FATHER AND SON

When his grief was spent, David longed to see his father. He decided to travel secretly, telling only Nathan of his plans. Dressing simply as a country dweller, he slipped away from the palace unnoticed, traveling to Bethlehem without an escort.

To the king's delight, he attracted no attention as he passed occasional fellow travelers on the road from Jerusalem to the place of his birth.

As he neared the small town nestled among the hills, a young shepherd dressed in sheepskin and sandals prodded a lazy bunch of sheep away toward the eastern slopes. Nothing had changed; the faces of his own generation had been replaced by those of the present generation, but life went as before.

David halted his mount and gazed off toward the spot on the nearest hill where the family altar still stood. It was there above that altar that he had seen his first vision—that of the crossed beams, the Lamb and the Shepherd-King—in the night sky! His pulse quickened. He could still hear the roar of the dragons and the angels' cries as they had clashed in battle in the heavens overhead! Then remembering his mission, he pressed on.

Once in Bethlehem, David dismounted and led his mule to the stable nearest Jesse's house where he left it in the care of a young stable hand.

His heart sang at simply being back in his hometown, the place of many warm and comforting memories. He spotted the tree on which he had practiced as a little boy with the new sling that his father had made for him. He walked over to the tree and ran his fingers over the familiar scars his own stones had made in its bark. To the right of the tree, and just a few yards away, was the home of the young lady with whom his brother Abinadab had fallen in love.

Lost in reverie, he turned toward his own ancient family home. David jumped when the door opened suddenly, bringing him back to the present.

"David, my son!" Jesse called in welcome, his sun-browned and wrinkled face breaking into a smile that softened the lines of care that the years had imprinted upon him. David, never noticing the wrinkles, thought again about how handsome his father was. As David held his father in his arms, Jesse became again for him—as he had been throughout David's childhood—his hero.

Their embrace was long and tight and accompanied only by exclamations of love and joy at being together again.

"Are you hungry, son?" Jesse asked quickly, remembering his manners as host when they finally let go of one another and entered the house. "You must be thirsty at least," he exclaimed, not waiting for David's reply to his first question.

Jesse hurried to the cupboard and brought out bread, cheese, and wine. He set out plates and cups and then pulled a knife from its leather pouch at his waist. With this he proceeded to deftly slice the bread and cheese. Meanwhile, David poured the wine. The two men fell upon the refreshments while happily catching up on all the news about other members of the family.

"By the way, Eliab has grown up a bit, David, and he regrets how cruelly he treated you as a youngster." And then, chuckling, he added, "In fact, he feels pretty foolish for telling you you'd never amount to anything! I hope you've forgiven him," Jesse said kindly.

Reflecting on his own heart, David could honestly say, "I never took offense, Father. Eliab was just...Eliab," he shrugged. "But I'm glad he has changed—for his family's sake!" David shifted in his chair and grew more serious.

"Actually, his taunt about my not amounting to anything was very true—except for God's mercy and favor," David said quietly, a sadness stealing over his face as he remembered his past sins. Then, after a brief pause, David smiled at his dad and changed the subject.

David's Purpose

"Father, I came to ask you a question—a serious question—and to give you some news that perhaps only you can understand."

"And it is...?" queried Jesse, urging him to continue.

David paused, wondering how to begin, then decided to simply get right to the point of his visit.

"Have you ever seen visions and dreamed dreams—about God?" David earnestly asked, hoping his father wouldn't think him irreverent for considering such a thing!

Without looking at David, Jesse finished chewing the bread he had just bitten off and washed it down with the remaining wine in his cup. After wiping his mouth with the back of his hand, he cleared his throat and looked squarely at David.

"Yes, my son," he answered carefully. "I have seen strange sights and dreamed wonderful dreams so sacred I've told no one of them until this moment. Even now I am not sure they should be discussed."

Jesse continued looking intently into David's eyes. "Why do you ask?"

"Because I have as well and have told no one for the same reasons you have not." David paused to push his empty plate and cup to the side, then leaned toward his father. "But I felt in my spirit that if there was anyone who could understand, it would be you.

"It was you who taught me to love Jehovah—that He was a heavenly Father who would gently lead me all the days of my life and that I could trust Him. From the day I was born, I heard His praises sung by you." David's eyes softened as he remembered. "You had a relationship with Him that I saw in few others as I was growing up and from which I drank deeply all through childhood."

Then David stopped and took a deep breath. "Father," he blurted out, "I have seen the King of kings, the One God will send to bring justice and peace to this world!"

"What?" Jesse exclaimed. "The Son of Promise? You have seen Him? Where? How can this be?" The old man jumped to his feet in his excitement.

"Now, hold on, Father!" David said, settling Jesse down. "I haven't seen Him with my *physical* eyes, but with my spiritual eyes."

Jesse thought that over and then slowly nodded. "That I can understand, son. So, tell me about Him!" he asked eagerly.

David described to his father the vision he had seen when he was 12 years old, and then each subsequent spiritual visitation of the Lamb and the Shepherd-King that he had had. Jesse was enthralled with the images and nodded knowingly at each.

"I saw Him as a heavenly King, Father," he soberly explained, "but one which will suffer greatly at our very own hands! The Holy One will become a sacrificial Lamb. We who should know better will treat him odiously!" David said with great anxiety in his voice. "That thought is so hard to bear!"

Before Jesse could echo his son's grief, David continued. "Our sins will kill Him, I just know it, and that fact breaks my heart!" David stood suddenly to his feet and began pacing the room. "I feel that my own sins of recent days have already begun that process!"

Then dropping back into his chair he said slowly, stressing each word, "I could not bear my own life if I weren't assured of His forgiveness. The consequences of my sins upon my entire family will be grievous enough—but if there were no forgiveness, not even death would bring release."

At this, David's eyes filled with tears as he looked pleadingly at his father for understanding.

"David," said Jesse softly, "I see the Lamb's eyes too, in every sacrifice I offer to Jehovah." Putting his hand gently on his son's arm that was resting on the table between them, he said, "I know we're forgiven. But I have also believed for some time that there will come a much greater sacrifice someday. What we have known in the past has only been a shadow of what is in God's ultimate plan for dealing with sin."

Shaking his head from side to side, he continued, "These little lambs we offer can never break the power of our sin!" Then, hitting his knee for emphasis, Jesse nearly shouted, "They only remind us of our need! So it doesn't surprise me that One sent from God Himself will have to die to set us free. We are such an impossible people and our sins are so great!" Jesse grimaced.

The men fell silent. Words ceased. Father and son were both lost in dreams of the Lamb who could take away their sins and change their hearts forever! But that such a Lamb-turned-King should have to die before He could rule—killed by their very own evil—was a strange and sorrowful thought indeed.

David finally broke the silence. Drawing himself up straight in his chair, he spoke with passion and great conviction.

"He loves us, Father! I have seen the love in His eyes! Such love will pay any price required to redeem us and defeat the dragons in our lives! Such love will melt the hardest heart!

And, I don't know how He will do it, but this Lamb will live again and rule His people in peace."

Silence, bathed in awe, again fell between them for what seemed a very long time.

"Father," continued David slowly after drawing a deep breath, "I have seen the self-worship in my own heart and felt the pain of separation from God that it brought to my soul. I have watched myself wound this King and others whom I love."

Pain swept David's face.

"But He has forgiven me, and I have surrendered my life to Him as never before," said the broken king, "and He has graciously given me another chance!"

At this, Jesse tenderly searched David's face and smiled sadly at the humility he saw in his son.

"It is strange," David went on reflectively, "I have always loved Him and known that He cared deeply for me, but never had I experienced His love in return as fully as when I felt His pain at my sin. Now He is more than life to me!" David's voice had dropped to a whisper as he poured out his heart to his father.

Leaning forward, David said with quiet forcefulness, "Now *He* is the King of Israel, not I. The throne is *His*. The anointing and power are *His*. The future and my life are *His* to do with as *He* wills! I care only that He be worshiped, and that the hearts of our people seek and serve Him alone," finished David fervently.

"Do you understand all this, Father?" David questioned Jesse with urgency.

"Yes, yes!" his father quickly responded, reassuringly touching his son's arm again.

David continued. "I had thought wrongly that houses and lands and wives and conquests in His name were glorious gifts

I could give Him. But I know now that all He wants is my heart!"

More News

Then, looking up, joy suddenly replacing the sorrow on his face as he remembered the other reason he had come to see his father, David went on. "And here is the news I came to give you: God has told me that the throne of the House of David will be established forever!"

As the news slowly sank into Jesse's heart, the king was overtaken by fresh revelation! "Could it be that someday the Shepherd-King will be born into our very own family line?" he asked incredulously. "Will the suffering Savior and coming King also be a Lion of Judah as well as a Lamb?" Wonder filled both father and son.

As they sat there quietly reflecting upon all they had shared that extraordinary afternoon, there flashed before them both the vision of the golden throne in the heavens upon which sat the King and the Lamb! Speechless and in awe at the sight they dropped to their knees and bowed before the Lord their God.

Plans for the Night

They remained in worship until the room began to grow dim in the deepening twilight. David then rose to his feet, brushing his hand across his eyes and standing tall. Without a word he headed for the door to take his leave. His father, stoop-shouldered yet stately, followed him to the threshold. He reached out and touched his son's shoulder to restrain him for a moment more.

"Your old room is just as you left it, David. Will you spend the night here with me?"

"Well," said David, turning and putting his arm lovingly around his father's shoulders, "I have another plan. Since no one has recognized me, I really want to play the part of a shepherd boy just one more time and sleep out under the stars." Glancing at the star-spangled sky and the full moon overhead, the king's heart skipped a beat. He smiled.

"As I arrived, I saw a young boy herding his sheep out to the range where I used to take mine. I think I'll tag along and do some pretending." They both laughed at the thought of the King of Israel playing shepherd in the hills around the little town of Bethlehem in the middle of the night!

After embracing once more and saying their final good-byes, David went back to the stable to get his bedroll and lyre.

A Strange Urge

Entering the stable and smelling the fresh straw that had just been scattered about for the animals to sleep upon, David had a sudden and strange urge to stay the night right there in the stable! But when the animal odors assaulted his senses as well, he quickly shook the notion from his head.

Imagine! David chuckled to himself, smiling delightedly. *A king sleeping in a smelly stable with the animals!* But even as he laughed at the thought, something inexplicable stirred within his spirit.

David paused for a moment, puzzled. Then, shrugging his shoulders, he picked up his gear and left, closing the door securely behind him.

WHEN DECEPTION REIGNS

"Sing for me, sir," begged Jonathan, the sandal-footed shepherd boy, after he and David had swapped lamb and lion stories and eaten supper together. So around the crackling campfire under the stars, the king-in-disguise sang and played long into the night.

Some melodies made the lad laugh, while others moved him to tears with their sad and haunting strains. But his favorite was, of course, the one about the good shepherd. Tenderly and lovingly David sang it as his fingers drew the delicate melody forth from the seasoned strings of his childhood lyre.

The Lord is my shepherd, I shall not be in want.
He makes me lie down in green pastures,
He leads me beside quiet waters,
He restores my soul.

He guides me in paths of righteousness
For His name's sake.

Even though I walk through the valley
Of the shadow of death,
I will fear no evil,
For You are with me;

Your rod and Your staff,
They comfort me.

You prepare a table before me
In the presence of my enemies.
You anoint my head with oil;
My cup overflows.

Surely goodness and love will follow me
All the days of my life!

And I will dwell in the house of the Lord
Forever.[1]

Jonathan and David finally retired to their bedrolls around midnight. How this Jonathan reminded David of his dear Jonathan of the past, Saul's slain son! What memories swirled around his heart!

Finally, however, like the boy, the king fell asleep. And although they had just met, they were in each other's dream, bound together in spirit by the ties that only shepherds understand.

When Jonathan awoke in the morning, to his disappointment, David was already gone. But the sweet strains of his music hung in the air around the young shepherd for many days to come.

Back to Ruling

There was a message from Joab when David reached Jerusalem.

My lord, the king,
I have fought against Rabbah and taken its water sup-
ply. Now muster the rest of the troops and besiege the

---

1   Psalm 23.

*city and capture it. Otherwise I will take the city, and
it will be named after me.*[2]

That very nearly sounds like a threat, mused David when
he had read Joab's message. *I wonder what it would take for Joab
to find power apart from my service?* Furrows deepened on his
forehead at the thought of Joab turning against him.

"On the other hand, he must be very weary of doing my
dirty work for me. I owe that man my life many times over!"
said the king, reflectively.

Then rolling the message up quickly and thrusting it into
the purse at his waist, he added earnestly, "I only wish he
could see with spiritual eyes what I have seen! Then earthly
power would not be such a consuming passion to him."

As David set about making plans to do as Joab had sug-
gested, he breathed a somber prayer. "God, help me if I ever
become weak in that great warrior's eyes!"

David the Father

As Joab had predicted a year before, after that campaign
there came a period of rest for the Israelite army.

Over the course of the next ten years, David watched as
his sons grew to be men, and his daughters, lovely young
women. Whenever he could, he shared the faith of his fathers
with his children, longing to see in their eyes the abandon-
ment to the love of God that he himself knew.

More often, however, all he saw—especially in his older
sons—was the same self-worship that had pitched him down
when he wasn't much older than they.

Nevertheless, David loved them deeply. Knowing what
Nathan had prophesied about the calamity that would someday come upon his own family from within, he clung to every

---

2   Second Samuel 12:27b-28.

moment of joy he had with them. He somehow hoped that the day of reckoning would never arrive. There was simply no way in which he could adequately prepare for it.

Trapped by the Past

David continued to see only the best in his children and had great difficulty dealing with the worst. On that awful day that the news reached him that his son Amnon had raped his own half-sister Tamar, David tore his clothes and wept—but did nothing whatsoever to punish Amnon or redeem Tamar's honor! He seemed paralyzed to act.

It was Absalom, Tamar's brother, who played the father-protector in his place. She went to live in his home, having been disgraced forever. As Absalom daily saw her sorrow, revenge grew in his heart...and respect for his father slowly died.

It took two years to find the right moment in which he could see that Amnon was killed, but the opportunity at last came. At his order, Absalom's men struck Amnon down with the sword, exacting discipline his own way.

David wept bitterly at the news and over the loss of his son. Absalom fled to Geshur, where he remained for three years. And David again did nothing to bring resolution.

Only Nathan had an inkling of why the great king was so helpless to bring justice and discipline to his own family. Besides David, only Nathan knew that their sins were the reaping of what David himself had sown in killing Uriah and taking his wife all those long years ago. Only Nathan suspected the depth of David's suffering as he watched the horrors of sin among those he loved most. Only Nathan knew that David carried the responsibility for it all upon his own shoulders.

Root of Rebellion

After the murder, Absalom grew comfortable with the rebellion that was rooted deep in his own heart. When Joab persuaded David to allow Absalom to come home to Jerusalem, the young man returned with a hunger for power and revenge that gnawed at his very soul. He would settle for no less than his father's overthrow.

By David's receiving him once again, Absalom regained access to the palace and renewed respectability before the people, both of which he needed in order to pursue his plan.

Serious Questions

"How long, Nathan," asked David sadly, "will it be before he draws the people off to himself like a pied piper? Will it be this year that he turns the sword upon me?" David heaved a sigh and turned wearily away from the window from which he had been watching the popular and handsome Absalom give counsel near the gates of the city. "His heart is set like flint against me, yet his words are as smooth as butter. I have never seen such calculated treachery!" Lifting his eyes to seek Nathan's he asked quietly, "What manner of man is this son of mine, Nathan?"

Nathan was relieved that David was finally willing to face the fact that Absalom was up to no good, but it broke his heart to see his king so miserable.

"As to your first question, you probably have a little more time, but not much," replied Nathan. "He'll make his move within a year, I think. From the look in his eye, he does not quite have as much support as he thinks necessary to ensure his success." David motioned Nathan to take a seat near him across the room from the open window as he summoned an attendant to bring them something cool to drink.

"He knows that you will not move against him," the prophet continued as he sat down in the ornate, high-backed chair, "so he can afford to sow more subversion before acting."

Rubbing his hand across his eyes, David softly asked another question: "When he says that there are injustices under my rule that grieve him, is he speaking the truth? Am I an unjust monarch?"

Nathan quickly answered. "David, you have ruled wisely and with great mercy. You think only of others and have been a constant example of devotion to God. You have never craved power nor used it to advance yourself or take revenge. He of all people should know that!" David's advisor leaned toward the king and spoke every word emphatically, yet tenderly. "Do you believe me, David?"

The king nodded slowly. "Thank you, Nathan," he said, sounding relieved.

"He feigns grief at supposed injustices in order to urge men to imagine that they exist and that his only goal is to champion them in their downtrodden condition!" By now Nathan was standing. The subject irritated him and he began pacing the floor in front of the king, continuing his response to David's questions.

"The man seems to have absolutely no conscience!" he blurted out.

"How easily deceived we are when we become a law unto ourselves," said David with a wince. "I was once in that pit myself, as you well know." His voice trailed off.

Rising to his feet as well, and then moving a bit unsteadily back toward the window, David asked one final question of the sage. "Nathan, could God be through with me? Could this be his way to remove me from the throne?"

Leaning forward with his hands firmly planted upon the sill, he added, "Authority is God's to give and take as He wills. The throne is His, as is any earthly power that comes with it."

Before Nathan could respond, David turned back to face him where he stood riveted to the floor in the center of the small room. "I would hand him the throne on a silver platter, except that I know in my heart that he has not the will nor vision to see to it that the Temple of God be built!" The color was rising in David's face. "Herein lies my struggle."

Chapter Twenty-one

HARD CHOICES

Within four years of his return, Absalom made his move. He sought an audience with the king.

"Your Majesty," said Absalom, bowing low before David with a feigned show of humility and allegiance. "May I make a request of my father, the king?"

"Of course, my son," answered David, a lump forming in his throat. How he longed to throw his arms around Absalom and tell him of his love for him! Surely, he thought, the wrongs could yet be made right!

But David remained frozen to his throne, knowing in his heart that Absalom would only despise him for displaying such emotion.

Absalom cleared his throat and, evading his father's direct gaze, continued in controlled tones, "Let me go to Hebron and fulfill a vow I made to the Lord. While I was living at Geshur in Aram, I made this vow: 'If the Lord takes me back to Jerusalem, I will worship the Lord in Hebron.' "

It was as though a knife were thrust through David's heart. He knew instinctively that Absalom was not going to Hebron to worship, but rather to declare himself king! That he would attempt to make God his accomplice galled David.

David held himself in check, silently crying out to God for wisdom. "Go in peace," David finally replied, keeping his regal bearing all the while.

Trying to conceal his delight, Absalom bowed once more and then quickly left the king's presence. After he was gone,

David slumped over on the throne, his head in his hands, and wept.

Preparing to Leave

"Bathsheba," said David softly, as he held her in his arms that night, "Absalom means to declare himself king at Mt. Hebron, maybe as early as tomorrow."

"Oh, David, has it come to this?" she drew the covers up tightly under her chin, as though to keep out the chill of what might be ahead of them. "And will you have to strike down your own son?" she whispered into the darkness.

David pushed off his own covers and got out of bed. After pacing the floor for a few minutes, he went to the window and looked out at the city. But through his tears, everything seemed to be drowning in a sea of gray.

"I honestly don't know what will be required of me," he answered in a wavering voice. "But there is no way that I could strike him down. Besides," he continued, "I don't know how great his following is yet. It may be I who is in danger of being stricken down, not he!"

David walked back to the bed and sat down in the stiff, decorative chair next to her side of the bed. Bathsheba reached out from under the covers to take his hand. She squeezed it gently.

"You will show him mercy to the very end, won't you?" she said, searching his face. "And if there is a choice between his life and yours, you will give yours to spare his! Am I not right, my dear David?" Bathsheba probed gently.

He didn't need to answer. Instead he cried, "If only he would forgive, the bitterness would go away! No crown can bring the freedom he has thrown away by harboring revenge!"

Then with an intensity beyond any Bathsheba had seen in David before, he said, "Nathan's prophecy did not indicate that either of us must die! If only he will repent and ask for mercy before something dreadful happens!"

After tucking her hand back under the warm covers, David rose slowly and returned to the window.

"In any event, we must all prepare to leave Jerusalem tomorrow," David said resolutely. "I don't want this city destroyed because of me."

Tilting his head back to look at the starless sky as he leaned against the window sill, he prayed.

"O Lord, preserve my life; in Your righteousness, bring me out of trouble, for I am Your servant. Surround me with songs of deliverance! Let me hear Your voice again."

From the bed came muffled sounds of weeping.

Flight of the Faithful

The royal household—including all David's wives, children, and many of the servants—prepared the next morning to travel. Supplies were packed and mules loaded. The army mustered for orders and government officials and advisors made their choices as to whom to follow: David or Absalom. Their royal monarch threatened no one and welcomed anyone who wanted to come.

David thought nothing of himself, yet when he and his family left Jerusalem for their safety, he was far from alone. A great multitude followed him out of the city, and more joined them as they traveled. Soldiers from surrounding territories joined his fighting men, pledging allegiance to the beloved king.

The priests Zadok and Abiathar—as well as all the Levites who served before the Ark of the Covenant—came with David as well, carrying the Ark at the front of the exodus. When some distance from Jerusalem, they stopped and offered sacrifices to God until everyone supporting David was out of the city. The smoke rising from the altar could be seen for miles around.

However, Ahithophel, one of David's trusted counselors, had gone over to Absalom and remained in Jerusalem.

David was concerned for many of the others and encouraged them to leave him, but no one would. When David saw that Ittai the Gittite was among them, he drew him aside.

"Why should you come along with us?" he asked. "Go back and stay with King Absalom," he gently urged. "You are a foreigner, an exile from your homeland. Why, you came only yesterday!" said David incredulously. "And today shall I make you wander about with us, when I do not know where I am going?" After a brief pause, David urged Ittai again, "Go back, and take your countrymen as well. May kindness and faithfulness be with you!"

But Ittai's reply reflected the commitment of everyone in that vast retinue. "As surely as the Lord lives, and as my lord the king lives, wherever my lord the king may be, whether it means life or death, there will your servant be." Such was the love of the people for King David.

The massive migration of people moved slowly through the countryside toward the desert, while those along the way wept as they passed by.

Only the Ark returned to Jerusalem at David's order, after the sacrifices were completed, accompanied by the priests Zadok and Abiathar and their two sons. The boys were commissioned to run messages to him, keeping him informed of what was happening in Jerusalem.

As David finished his instructions to the priests, he added gravely, "If I find favor in the Lord's eyes, He will bring me back and let me see it and His dwelling place again." Then with a catch in his voice, he continued, "But if He says, 'I am not pleased with you,' then I am ready; let Him do to me whatever seems good to Him." Sadly Zadok and Abiathar embraced the shepherd-king and then prepared to leave for Jerusalem.

As the Ark faded from sight beyond the hills, David lifted his face toward Heaven, his eyes unable to see because of his tears.

"O Lord!" he prayed. "How I love the house where You live, the place where Your glory dwells!"

Hope Mixed With Despair

Slowly he turned northward, facing the rugged brush- and rock-covered Mount of Olives that rose before him. Removing his sandals and drawing the folds of his robes up and over his head in humility before God, he began its ascent, weeping as he went. Soon all in that great company did the same, all of one mind and heart with their king.

As he trudged up the hillside, he remembered that the defector Ahithophel would now be advising Absalom. Instantly David prayed, "O Lord, turn Ahithophel's counsel into foolishness."

At the summit, whom should he find waiting for him but Hushai, an old and dear advisor of his and his father's before him! Hushai's robe was torn and his head covered with dust, in mourning for this dark day of betrayal. As old as he was, he still wanted to march with David!

"Dear Hushai," began the king, "I can't let you come with us! It will be too difficult and dangerous!"

Then seeing the sudden droop of Hushai's shoulders and the sorrow in his eyes, David had another thought.

"My friend, I know what you can do that may be of more benefit than your slaying a thousand men." David couldn't conceal the hope that was springing into his eyes. "Go to Jerusalem and pretend to be Absalom's servant. Gain his confidence and then give him counsel that will frustrate that given by Ahithophel."

He and David talked further in low tones, and then Hushai bowed low to the ground before the king. David drew him gently to his feet and bid him farewell.

David's Prayer

Alone at last on the summit of the Mount of Olives, David dropped to his knees and began to pour his love out to the God of his life.

"Whom have I in Heaven but You? And being with You, I desire nothing on earth!"

Struggling for words, he made his plea. "O Lord, defend my cause! Do not take away my soul along with sinners, my life with bloodthirsty men in whose hands are wicked schemes!" he cried. "O Lord, redeem me and be merciful to me! In You alone do I put my hope!"

And then, as peace stole over his soul, he turned to face Jerusalem again, his eyes fixed upon the barren hills over which the precious Ark had passed. In but a whisper, he prayed:

"O dear Lord, bring me again before Your presence! Let the morning bring me word of Your unfailing love, for I have put my trust in You."

David prayed long into the night, while the people slept on the hillside below him.

Chapter Twenty-two

THE BATTLE

The next day, their journey toward the safety of the desert beyond the Jordan River took them near the city of Bahurim.

Ambush

Thud! A stone hit David in the back! Then another struck the captain of his guard. The next moment, a shower of dirt and stones rained down upon the king and those positioned closest to him! The orderly procession came to a sudden and confused halt, everyone turning this way and that trying to see from where the barrage was coming!

Swords began flashing in the morning sun; laden mules stomped restlessly behind the front guard; tempers were rising.

Then an angry, bitter voice rang out from somewhere beyond the boulders along the roadside. One of the soldiers identified him as Shimei, a relative of King Saul.

"Curse you, David!" he shouted. "Get out, get out, you man of blood, you scoundrel!" After throwing another stone that barely missed David's head, he continued his verbal assault. "The Lord has repaid you for all the blood you shed in the household of Saul, in whose place you have reigned. The Lord has handed the kingdom over to your son Absalom, hasn't He?" A jagged rock hit David in the shoulder, making him stumble. "You have come to ruin because you are a man of blood!"

The words pierced David's heart! He absorbed then without defense.

However, his men were outraged!

Abishai, his face red with indignation, pleaded with David, "Why should this dead dog curse my lord the king? Let me go over and cut off his head!"

At this, every officer instinctively moved into an offensive position around David, ready to attack at the first signal from the king.

But to their amazement, David's hand quickly reached out to restrain Abishai, his friend of many years. "Don't you see, Abishai, if he is cursing because the Lord said to him 'Curse David,' who can ask, 'Why do you do this?' "

Stunned silence struck everyone within hearing distance. Shaking their heads in disbelief, the men sheathed their swords. They couldn't believe their ears! *What kind of reasoning is this?* each asked himself without speaking.

David continued slowly, searching their faces. "My son, who is of my own flesh, is trying to take my life! Why not this Benjamite!" David's voice then rose as he called out clearly for everyone to hear, "Leave him alone; let him curse, for the Lord has told him to!"

Then quietly, more to himself than to the men, he added, "It may be that the Lord will see my distress and repay me with good for the cursing I am receiving today."

Bewildered, yet sensing again in this strange moment the anointing of God upon their shepherd-turned-king, they did the only thing they could do—shielded David with their own bodies, taking the blows along with their beloved king.

New Songs

And so they moved down the roadway in silence, their faces set toward the horizon. The only sounds were of marching feet, punctuated by the vitriolic curses of the lone figure madly hurling stones and dirt at the king from his position on the hills above them.

However, something happened that day to those around David who chose to share his suffering with him, not just tolerate it. They found new songs rising within their hearts that, amazingly, drowned out the bitterness in Shimei's voice! And they actually began to feel sorry for him.

As for David, his eyes were fixed not on the desert ahead, but on his memory of yet another Shepherd-King from long ago, who called to him from crossed beams in the sky.

But to Joab, the scene was senseless. If David was to rule, he should crush everyone and anyone within his path. As one of David's commanders, he felt humiliated that he was not allowed to silence this opposition with the blade.

"I'm sick of righteousness!" Joab muttered to himself. "I don't understand in the least leaders who seek to rule through submission, whether the cause is just or not!"

Sometime during that hot afternoon, Shimei quit, having spent his venom in the only way he knew. He slipped out of sight and returned to his own house to brag about the power he had displayed over the "Mighty King of Israel"!

David and all those with him arrived at day's end physically and emotionally exhausted. For some, however, the songs born in their spirits on that unusual day would play on in their dreams that night, as angels danced to the music.

On the other hand, those who had difficulty trusting this God of David's would find only dragons in their sleep.

His Reflection

They camped by a spring that supplied clear, fresh water to a small stream that meandered through the hills in that part of the country.

As David bent down to wash in the brook, he caught a glimpse of his own reflection in the water. What was in his eyes? He withdrew his hands and waited for the water's surface to become smooth again.

That look! When had he seen it before? "Ah," he remembered aloud. "It was right after I killed the lion that was attacking my sheep. I was bending over a stream much like this one when I saw in my eyes..." he looked hard at himself again.

"...the eyes of the King who will die upon the beams someday!" In awe, he saw the eyes again, although set now in a very much older and wiser face. Shifting back on his heels, he tried to reconstruct the feelings of that day when he was 17.

"Oh, yes, I wondered then if I would someday feel the Lamb's pain..." he whispered. "Did I feel it today? And did my silent suffering set someone free?" he asked himself.

How he wished he could know!

Changes

The king's heart beat differently these days, with a deeper yearning for Heaven and a greater sense of his own dependence upon God. As he sat outside his tent that night, with his lyre resting upon his knee, he was lost in thought...about winning and losing.

His definition of victory had been changing, slowly but surely. Victory no longer had anything to do with intrigue, politics, or taking captives and plunder. It had more to do with forgiveness and mercy!

And is not the greatest victory found in being able to receive blows without retaliation, and letting a guilty man live when he cries for mercy? he pondered inwardly. And then, as he wrung his own hands and shook his head sadly, he wistfully ventured aloud, "If only I had understood earlier how much my own heart would need forgiveness, perhaps less blood would be on these hands!" He gazed at them, now spread out, palms up before him. "Mercy is often the last lesson to be learned," he whispered as he turned his eyes to the sky.

He heaved a long sigh and then smiled wryly at the thought of Joab hearing him speak such "foolishness."

The Pain Continues

Back in Jerusalem, David's plan was working. Hushai's advice would be naively received above Ahithophel's—but not until after Absalom had violated each of David's concubines. This he did in broad daylight on the rooftop of the palace, in the sight of all Israel, in order to humiliate David and solidify his own authority among those who remained. It was just as Nathan had predicted over 20 years ago!

And so was God's judgment against David for his sin with Bathsheba at last satisfied. Ironically, with this despicable action, Absalom unwittingly moved King David one step closer to freedom.

Battle Plan

Ahithophel's military plan for overthrowing David in battle involved shedding only David's blood and bringing the rest of the people back to Jerusalem. On the other hand, Hushai's plan called for massive slaughter and heroic victory.

Absalom, in his pride and lust for power, chose Hushai's bloody plan! Playing up to Absalom's brutal nature, Hushai's counsel confounded the counsel of Ahithophel, just as David had hoped and prayed it would. In all-out battle the insurgents would be no match for David's seasoned troops.

Within hours, Zadok's and Abiathar's sons had found David and given him details of the plan, along with instructions from Hushai that would put David in an excellent fighting position.

David proceeded to divide his massive troops into three contingencies to be led by his best commanders. He himself intended to march with them. But the response from his commanders deeply touched David's heart.

"No, my lord, you must not go out with us! If we are forced to flee, they won't care about us," insisted Abishai, stabbing the point of his sword into the ground for emphasis. "Even if half of us die, they won't care!" But then with a tenderness uncommon for soldiers on the field, he continued, "But you are worth ten thousand of us!" Looking respectfully but resolutely at David, he added, "It would be better for you to give us support from Mahanaim."

Ittai nodded his own approval of the plan and then said earnestly, "You alone are God's anointed! You must be alive tomorrow to lead your people, O king."

"Yes, my lord, we all agree," joined in Joab forcefully, secretly wanting David out of the way so that no mercy would need to be shown.

As much as he longed to fight alongside them, David knew that they were right. He would remain in Mahanaim as they advised.

"But there is one thing I ask of you," David said firmly, "and that is, be gentle with Absalom...for my sake."

Abiathar's and Ittai's eyes softened in consent. Joab merely gritted his teeth.

Undone

The armies met near the Forest of Ephraim and then spread out over the countryside. The battle was intense and 20 thousand fell that day. Absalom's forces were defeated soundly by David's on all sides, both in the field and in the forest. It was suspected that many of Absalom's unseasoned soldiers defected, hiding in the forest to escape death by the sword.

It was there in the forest, in fact, that Absalom found himself undone—by his own crowning glory—his thick and lustrous hair that became entangled in the branches of a tree!

And it was Joab himself who defied David's request and ran him through with not just one javelin, but three, as he hung by his hair from the branches.

The body was hastily cut down by Joab and his men and thrown into a deep pit. Rocks were piled upon the body to hide it.

Joab then sounded the trumpet signaling victory.

But the day suddenly lost its color as news of Joab's deed was whispered from soldier to soldier. The sky turned gray and fear spread through the ranks. What would David do? How could Joab have defied the king? How could this horror be assuaged? What manner of "victory" was this?

Shadows of Death

Back in Mahanaim, David's heart skipped a beat at the moment of the brutal slaying, and a dark foreboding came upon him. Shadows of death blanketed his spirit.

"Have we lost the battle?" he tensely asked himself, his brow deeply furrowed, his palms damp with cold sweat. "Has something happened to my son?" He could bear to think no further.

Suddenly the watchmen on the wall called out, "A runner is coming!"

Hope sprang up in David's heart. "If he is alone, he must have good news!"

But then the watchman saw another runner approaching, overtaking the first. Still, the king hoped for a good report.

As he awaited the runners' messages, David steadied himself against the nearest wall of the city, his legs nearly buckling beneath him.

Chapter Twenty-three

ABSALOM, MY SON!

Blindly David half ran, half stumbled away from the messengers who had brought the news of his own victory—and Absalom's death. Up the worn stone steps to the little room over the gateway, the closest place to be alone, David laboriously climbed, heaving great sobs of grief as he went.

"O my son Absalom! My son, my son Absalom!" David cried out. "If only I had died instead of you—O Absalom, my son, my son!" His tortured cries carried far beyond the courtyard and the city walls, filling even the innocent with shame at Joab's guilt and David's sorrow.

The young men who had brought the news were shocked and dumbfounded! Sinking to the ground beside the wall—exhausted and unrewarded for their run—they stared in disbelief at one another, struggling to grasp the significance of Absalom's death to David. But they couldn't, for they were young and had no sons of their own, nor the regrets that their great king had.

As for the fighting men, many of them struggled to understand as well. Why this burden of a common guilt, as though they had each had a hand in the crime? they wondered.

Joab was simply disgusted. It mattered little that his own disobedience to the king had triggered this crisis. He saw only that his men were dishonored and ashamed of even being soldiers. This angered him.

Joab's Struggle

Exhausted, Joab threw himself down on his bedroll to take a nap while he waited for the rest of the troops to return from the field. But he had trouble sleeping. The memory of Absalom's cries awakened him every time he dozed off.

"Was the boy trying to beg for mercy when I ran him through?" he mumbled, rubbing his aching head. "Should I have given him an opportunity to surrender?" he asked himself, his conscience stirring within him.

But then his warrior mind overruled. *If he had been allowed to repent, David would have forgiven him—even after all the slaughter he has caused!* Angered at the thought, Joab got up from his bedroll, knowing that sleep was impossible.

"What are fighting men for, if not to kill our enemies before they kill us?" Joab growled, his blood rising. "The king's request was stupid!"

He grabbed his cloak and sandals. After putting them on at the door of his tent, Joab set off at a fast pace toward the desert and away from camp.

Can I serve this king any longer? he asked himself.

Then suddenly, fear struck. He stopped dead in his tracks. *Will David take revenge upon me for Absalom's death? Does he know yet that I am the one who killed him?* he wondered anxiously.

Memories

Then his mind went back to the early years and the great battles he and David had fought side by side. "What a mighty warrior!" Joab said aloud into the late afternoon sky as he studied the clouds overhead.

And other memories came back—memories of the mystical music of the poet-warrior as he had sung to them around the campfire at night while on campaigns against their enemies.

"How his melodies drew us all together," he murmured. "What strange devotion that man has to his God!" Then dropping

144

his gaze to the horizon where smoke from someone's altar was rising like silver wisps into the sky, he was struck by a sense of wonder. "One would think him a priest as much as a king!"

After a few moments, Joab kicked a stone absently with his foot and took a deep breath of the crisp, clean desert air. Then he resumed walking.

"Yes, David is my lord still. And I will fight for my position at his side as long as he has the strength to lead," he resolved then and there. "There is no one like David!"

"However," he added with a nervous laugh, "only if he doesn't kill me for running his rebellious son through!"

He turned around and faced his camp. With the sun behind him and low in the sky, he followed his own shadow as he slowly walked back.

"We are cut from different cloth, the king and I, but I will serve him as best I can, if he will let me."

Guilt by Association

By the time he reached his camp, all the armies had returned from the field and were awaiting orders. As he saw the effects of the weight of undeserved shame in their eyes, he began to fear that they, rather than David, would avenge Absalom's death and have his head!

So, at twilight, as they stole into the city like criminals—supposed victory having turned into defeat—Joab decided to speak to David immediately. Everyone needed resolution—and he needed to divert attention away from himself.

Besides, he thought indignantly, *we won! We saved his neck and he hasn't even had the decency to thank us!* His face was flushed with anger. *Come what may, this has got to end!* He set out to find David.

Words of Comfort

Meanwhile, when the messengers' news of Absalom's death reached Nathan's ears, he went looking for David, knowing the king would be in torment. The cries he heard as he left his house and entered the street of the city confirmed his worse fears.

He followed the sound of the cries. When he reached the closed doorway of the little room over the gateway, to which David had withdrawn, he knocked gently.

"David, it is I, Nathan. Please let me in."

When there was no response, only muffled sobs and groaning, Nathan pushed the door ajar just enough to see David face down on the floor. The old door squeaked on its rusty hinges.

Nathan dropped to his knees beside the man whose heart he knew better than anyone else, and he began to pray.

"God, remember David and all the hardships he has endured. Bind up his wounds and heal his broken heart, O Lord!" Nathan's gravelly voice spoke as tenderly as David had ever heard it. The king's sobbing eased, but his shoulders still heaved.

Nathan continued praying. "Let him see Your face again. Restore the fortunes of this servant who loves you better than life," pleaded Nathan, his voice choked with emotion.

"O God, bring to an end his suffering. May Your plans be fulfilled for him." Nathan fell silent.

Strengthened by Nathan's loving prayer, David then spoke through his tears, "Remember, O Lord, Your great mercy and love, for they are from of old." Then barely above a whisper, he asked one last time, "Remember not the sins of my youth and my rebellious ways; according to Your love remember me, for You are good, O Lord."

A soft breeze floated through the unshuttered window near him and exited through the open doorway. It was as if his burdens were being lifted and carried away on that breeze.

David heaved a sigh of relief. Somehow he knew now that the past was over and the reaping at an end.

"Everything's in His hands now, isn't it, Nathan?" David asked as he slowly rose to his feet and turned to face the Prophet. "I had thought I had surrendered everything before, but when Absalom died, I realized by my own grief that I had hoped yet to persuade God to intervene and do things my way."

Nathan nodded his understanding.

"But, Nathan, the pain!" David said, his voice laced with agony as memories flooded his heart. "If I had known the price of sin, would I have done it?" David queried himself and his friend.

After shaking his head slowly from side to side, David looked deep into Nathan's eyes and answered his own question, "I can't believe I would have, not if I had really understood!"

He brushed his hand over his eyes as though to remove some unseen veil, as one brushes away cobwebs encountered in the woods.

Then, looking beyond Nathan as though he weren't there, David said with passion, "How I love His laws now, for they are life to me! They guard my soul!"

The two men slowly left the little room and descended the worn stone steps to the ground together. Nathan took leave of the king when they reached the house in which David was staying until they could return to Jerusalem.

Joab's Plea

And so Joab found him there. Before David could ask any questions about his son's death, his commander intended to forge ahead on behalf of the fighting men who awaited word from the king. He cleared his throat and began.

"My lord, today you have humiliated all your men, who have just saved your life and the lives of your family," he said with abrupt intensity. David was startled.

Not having been stopped, Joab continued. "You love those who hate you and hate those who love you! You have made it clear today that the commanders and their men mean nothing to you." Joab tried to keep his voice under control. David was speechless and moved not a muscle as he heard Joab's indictment.

"I see that you would be pleased if Absalom were alive today and all of us were dead." Jarred back to reality with Joab's harsh words, David walked to the window and looked down upon the soldiers standing forlornly in the courtyard below. Conviction gripped him.

"Now go out and encourage your men," instructed Joab, seeing that his words were hitting their mark. "I swear by the Lord that if you don't go out, not a man will be left with you by nightfall. This will be worse for you than all the calamities that have come upon you from your youth till now."

At this final remark, David reached for his robe and strode from the house. Joab followed at a short distance.

David took his seat in the gateway at which signal the men gratefully came before him. Man by man they passed by him, searching his face for absolution, and they found it. David blessed and thanked each one.

His heart is with us again! each one said to himself, and the cloud of shame they had been under lifted and disappeared.

Honor Restored

The soldiers went to their beds that night with victory in their hearts. Their vigor and devotion to David, whose edges had become dull that awful day, were again sharp and ready for whatever service tomorrow might demand of them.

And David ended the day with his lyre upon his knee. As he reclined on the couch by his bed, he waited for the words and melody to come.

Suddenly, from years ago came the memory of a conversation he had had with Nathan on the roof of his palace. They had been trying to decide where to put the Ark of the Covenant in the already-crowded city.

With the shadow of Mt. Moriah behind him as they looked southward into the city, David had said matter-of-factly, "Obedience and devotion are the stuff of blessing, Nathan. Don't you think so?"

He hadn't realized at the time how significant that statement would be in the telling of his own life. How much he had learned on the subject!

Bending over his lyre, his fingers deftly inventing a new melody and his thoughts flying in harmony with each note, he began to sing:

> *Lord, Your laws*
> *Make this simple child wise*
> *Lord, Your precepts*
> *Give joy to my heart!*

> *Lord, Your commands*
> *Give light to these eyes*
> *Lord, Your laws*
> *Make this simple child wise!*

> *Pure and sure, altogether righteous*
> *More precious than gold*
> *Sweeter than honey, warn me and guide me*
> *Make my heart pure!*

Refrain:

O Lord, my rock
Make my heart pure!
O Lord, my redeemer
Make my heart pure!
Make my heart pure![1]

1   Adapted from Psalm 19:7-10.

Chapter Twenty-four

CROSSING THE JORDAN

In the days ahead, those who had followed Absalom remembered the deeds of their king of old...and had second thoughts.

"Wasn't David the one who rescued us from the hand of all our enemies? Shall we not return to him now that Absalom is dead?" these two-legged sheep who so easily followed hirelings said to one another, their allegiance shifting like the desert sand.

As for David's own tribe of Judah, their hearts were won over by their king as though they were one man. They sent word for the king and all who were with him to meet them at the Jordan River and they would bring their monarch home. So David and his family and all who had been in Mahanaim with him packed up and proceeded west to the banks of the Jordan. They would camp there until Judah arrived and helped them ford the river.

David's Longing

The day they reached the Jordan and set up camp to wait for Judah was beautiful, with a few fluffy clouds to give relief from the heat.

After everyone was settled, David strolled along the banks of that ancient flood. And as the last rays of the sun—red with promise of another glorious day tomorrow—touched the pulsing current of the Jordan River, David was amazed at the transformation before him. Beneath the dancing diamonds that sparkled on the peak of each wave in the setting sun, the tide turned an absolute, deep crimson!

"The mighty Jordan flows with blood!" David marveled. "But not with the blood that brings grief and loss, but the blood that redeems!" he stated with conviction, at the same time wondering how he knew...

In the next moment he recalled the lamb on the family altar of his childhood days—and then the Shepherd-King shedding His blood on the crossed beams—and it dawned on him that it was *their* blood that pulsed before him!

As he gazed in wonder at the crimson flow, the longing rose in his breast for all to know its power to set men free.

"I have been through this river and have been cleansed of my sin...and will likely need its cleansing again," he added ruefully. "But the journey to its banks is a precious privilege for me!"

"If only," he wistfully murmured, "the blood of the Lamb could be applied again to every household in Israel, as in Moses' day, so that eternal death would pass them by! Oh, that the people would seek His salvation!"

As the sun's reflection died away, overtaken by the somber hues of the night sky, the surging crimson current became once more a simple gray-brown river, quietly flowing within its ancient banks.

Different Eyes

The next day David looked at his people with the Lamb's eyes—forgiveness—the stuff of his life. When Shimei, the Benjamite who had cursed him so vehemently only a short time ago, appeared on the opposite bank with his kinsmen to beg for mercy, David saw him with different eyes. As the frightened Shimei forded the once crimson stream, David allowed the blood of the Lamb to cover him and his sin. And David forgave.

And Joab—his strangely loyal commander who was always fearfully taking matters into his own hands and who had killed his son Absalom—he forgave.

On the day of David's crossing the Jordan to reclaim the throne in Jerusalem, no blood was shed but the Lamb's.

Final Rebellion

The jealous in-fighting between Judah and the other tribes grieved David, and one last rebellion tested his call. Sheba, a Benjamite, drew off a following of Israelites in resistance to David's rule. But once Sheba's rebellion was quelled, David was established without dispute.

Only restitution to the Gibeonites, whom Saul had wronged, was left in order to settle issues of the past. This David accomplished by turning seven of Saul's descendants over to the Gibeonites. Mephibosheth alone, Jonathan's son whom David had promised to care for as his own and who had been living with the king since his father's death, was withheld.

Of course, David's old enemies the Philistines—like a thorn in his flesh—challenged his patience from time to time. But by God's grace, David's men prevailed in battle after battle.

Israel's Worship

The earthly shepherd-king sang a great deal during these years, and many of his songs were taken up by the singers who led in worship before the Ark of the Covenant. As he bowed his face to the ground in the presence of God, his own words— born in hardship as well as success—poured from the lips of the worshipers around him.

Find rest, O my soul, in God alone;
My hope comes from Him.

He alone is my rock and my salvation;
He is my fortress, I will not be shaken!

My salvation and my honor depend on God;
He is my mighty rock, my refuge.
Trust in Him at all times, O people;
Pour out your hearts to Him,

For God is our refuge.
Our hope is in Him![1]

Will they ever really understand what they are singing? he wondered. *Will they yield to the humbling hand of a loving God—a God who hates sin as much as He loves His people? Will they put their hope in Him alone?* The fear that they wouldn't filled him with dread for their future.

Strange Impulse

Times were good again for David, the warrior-king of all Israel. As he looked out across the land in all directions, he was king of all he could see and beyond. His massive armies kept peace, and he ruled the people with justice and mercy.

One morning, as David was meeting with Joab and his commanders in the palace throne room to evaluate their national military status, a strange impulse came over the king. Actually, it seemed quite natural...to wonder how many men of fighting age there might be in all Israel.

"How many do you think?" he curiously asked Joab.

His commander of many years fidgeted a bit. "Enough, my lord. More than enough!" he answered emphatically.

"Well, I want to know exactly," David insisted. "Listen, Joab," he continued excitedly, "we're not engaged in any major

---

1   Psalm 62:5-8.

154

skirmish right now, so you and your men could be free to travel the length and breadth of this great nation and count them!"

A look stole into David's eyes that scared Joab. "Why do you want to do such a thing?" Joab asked anxiously in response, trying to stall the king.

In a split second Joab remembered a scene similar to this one from nearly 30 years ago—when David had announced to his troops that he wanted to spend time in Jerusalem instead of leading them into battle in the spring. The look in his eyes was the same.

Joab glanced at the other men to see if they had misgivings. Seeing no sign of any, Joab uncomfortably shrugged his shoulders and acquiesced to the king. "As you wish, my lord."

"Good," smiled David. "Begin at once!" At this the men were dismissed.

Conviction Falls Again

Nine months later, at about the time the census was nearing completion, David awoke in the middle of the night with a throbbing pain in his head. He arose and sought fresh air above his chambers.

As he paced the courtyard that had been created on the palace roof, the pain left his head only to become lodged in his heart. His very spirit seemed oppressed!

It was another moonlit night. In his agony he fixed his gaze southward upon the city. His eye was caught by the shimmering water in the pool on top of Uriah's house, just as it had been 30 years ago.

He involuntarily shuddered. "What an arrogant young man I was!" the king said aloud with disgust.

He turned northward as if to put the past behind him, and searched for Mt. Moriah in the moonlight. He hoped that the vision of the temple that would someday be built there by his son Solomon would reappear and take his mind off this pain. But instead the Shepherd-King stood alone on its summit.

David anxiously sought His eyes. Oh, for the comfort of those gentle eyes! For the last several months, worship had been difficult. The courts of the Lord had turned into a desert for him. How thirsty he was for God's presence, which seemed increasingly distant!

"And now He has come to me!" exclaimed David, breathing a sigh of relief through his pain. But as he sought comfort from those eyes, he saw instead...sorrow and reproach!

The distraught king wrung his hands in agony. "What is wrong?" he whispered, searching his suddenly-stricken conscience for the source of his guilt. And then, as if by revelation, he understood.

"I have done it again! I have again acted arrogantly!" he cried out. "My eyes were filled with my own success and my heart with pride!" He bent over as the pain in his chest intensified.

"O my God," he fervently prayed, "what a fool I have been! Forgive me for thinking for a moment that my strength lay in how many fighting men I might have at my command!" he spoke into the crisp night air, his eyes on the Shepherd-King in the distance. "Forgive my sin and take away my guilt!"

Then, as he felt the loving arms of his Lord holding him close once again, he sobbed and sobbed like a child.

"My strength is only in You!" he whispered. "Without You, I am nothing, and no matter how many men there might be to fend off evil for me, I would be doomed. With You, I need no one else!"

While the rest of Jerusalem slept, David wept in the arms of his Sovereign Lord and Shepherd-King until the stars faded away in the gray light of morning. As he rose to go back to his chambers and prepare for the day, he looked into the sky and shivered.

"It's going to be a stormy day!" he said into the damp wind that was beginning to whip about the rooftops.

156

Chapter Twenty-five

THE FINAL SACRIFICE

Davids was right. It would be a stormy day—one of the darkest of his reign.

After breakfast, Gad, one of David's spiritual advisors, fought his way through the gale to the palace. He bore a dreadful message from God for the king.

Wet and windblown, Gad bowed before the penitent king. Then rising slowly, with a grim look on his tired face, he began:

"This is what the Lord says, 'I am giving you three options. Choose one of them for Me to carry out against you for your sin.' "

Silence fell between them. Then David spoke gently, "Go ahead, my friend. I deserve every blow. My sin has defiled the nation and punishment must come."

Gad slowly put God's options before the king. "Shall there be three years of famine, three months of fleeing from your enemies while they pursue you, or three days of plague? Think it over and decide how I should answer the One who sent me," he concluded, his voice husky with emotion from the weight of his mission and the awfulness of the choices.

David stood and walked weakly to the window now shuttered against the storm. He raised his hand as if to open it, then thought better of it and turned back to face the man of God. The king's face was ashen, and in his distress he had aged greatly in the space of a single day.

He sighed, the pain still piercing his heart. Gad waited patiently.

Finally the king answered wearily. "Let us fall into the hands of the Lord, for His mercy is great; but do not let me fall into the hands of men." Trying to muster courage, he said, barely audibly, "Therefore I choose...three days of plague in the land."

Without looking at Gad, David slumped against the wall by the shuttered window. Outside the storm raged. Gad slipped out unnoticed.

Facing Judgment

The plague afflicted 70 thousand men, women, and children from Dan to Beersheba during the three black days of judgment that followed. The storm heightened, the sky blackened by the natural and spiritual sorrow that blanketed the nation...and the heart of the shepherd-king.

David, broken and in inexpressible grief, climbed once again to his rooftop courtyard, shielding his eyes against the light rain that still fell, straining to see Mount Moriah through the mist. His heart nearly stopped beating at the sight before him!

Sword drawn toward Jerusalem, the fearsome avenging angel of the Lord stood riveted to the summit, upon the ancient threshing floor owned by Aranauh, the Jebusite! He was about to strike the inhabitants of the city with the plague that had already ripped through the countryside.

David, his sackcloth soaked and hanging awkwardly from his frame, called out in anguish to the Lord, "I am the one who has sinned and done wrong. O God, these are but sheep! What have they done?" In desperation he cried, "Let Your hand fall upon me and my family instead!" He sank to the watery gravel rooftop and lay prostrate before the Lord.

At the very moment that the avenging angel stretched out his hand to afflict Jerusalem, the Lord Himself cried out, "Enough! Withdraw your hand!" And as if there were a truce in the heavens, the violent storm began to subside.

David's Sacrifice

The next day brought southerly winds that began refreshing the sodden earth and Israel's aching spirit. In response to the Lord's orders given to him through Gad, David made his way quickly to the threshing floor above which the angel remained as if suspended between Heaven and earth. The king was to build an altar on the threshing floor and offer a sacrifice for his sins.

When Araunah saw him coming, he bowed down before David with his face to the ground. David bid him rise and then addressed him.

"Araunah, please let me have the site of your threshing floor so that I can build an altar to the Lord," David said to him gently. "It will stop the plague on the people! Sell it to me at the full price."

Araunah, filled with joy that the plague could be stopped and that he could be of help to the king, insisted, "Take it! Let my lord the king do whatever pleases him." Then thinking quickly of what else the king would need, he added, "I will give the oxen for the burnt offering, the threshing sledges for the wood, and the wheat for the grain offering. Take it all!"

Putting his hand on Araunah's shoulder, David spoke with great seriousness to his subject. "No, this must cost *me*, not you, my friend. I insist on paying the full price! I will not sacrifice a burnt offering that costs me nothing."

At that David paid Araunah a handsome price in gold for the site and all that he would need. As he sacrificed to the Lord, the Lord answered him with fire from Heaven on the altar!

And finally the plague was over. As David sank to his knees in worship on that now sacred site, the Lord ordered the angel to put his sword back into its sheath.

Forgiven

That night the weary king dreamed of a river—a simple river that surged with the blood of the Lamb of God. As he hurried to its banks and plunged into its waters, the burden of the sorrows of his sin and the people's suffering were carried away!

Then he fell into a deep and dreamless sleep. By morning, the pain in his heart was gone.

As he threw open the shutters of his bedroom and looked out toward the summit of Mt. Moriah—which he now owned—his heart raced with plans of the temple that would be in that exact location. He must begin preparation!

Chapter Twenty-six

A KINGDOM NOT OF THIS WORLD

A deeply sobered David ruled his people from then on, his vision set on the heavens and the Kingdom to come rather than on himself. His graying hair, ever curly, crowned a face etched by heartache but graced by eyes of mercy. As he had been forgiven, he increasingly forgave.

His remaining sons, Adonijah and Solomon, were grown and as different as night and day. Adonijah was independent and selfish, shortsighted and disdainful of instruction. Solomon was sensitive and introspective, in awe of life and grateful for the love and instruction of his father.

Adonijah reminded David of his own brother Eliab, and he hoped that time would season the boy as it had his brother. To avoid conflict, David let Adonijah grow as he pleased. And into Solomon he poured his heart.

Father and Son

Solomon loved the poetry and songs his father composed—crafted from the timber of his experiences and his deep passion for God.

"Father, sing for us," begged Solomon after he and his mother had spent a rare and delightful evening with the king over a sumptuous meal and much reminiscing. "Put to music that story you used to tell us kids about how blessed the children of a righteous man will be!" he lovingly teased his father.

"Oh, you like that one, do you?" replied his father, stroking his beard and furrowing his brow in mock puzzlement.

Then breaking into a warm smile—with a wink in Bathsheba's direction—he reached for his lyre, which was placed each evening near the couch where he would recline after dinner.

"My lord," Bathsheba remonstrated when she eyed the worn and battered lyre he held so dear, "you really must have a new lyre designed for you!" Then laughingly she added, "You look like a country shepherd boy when you hold that old thing in your arms! I half expect a flock of sheep to wander in from the desert every time you play!"

David stroked its smooth wooden frame tenderly and then tested each string, adjusting the thumbsets when needed.

"I wish they *would* wander in! How wonderful to feel their soft wool again and see the simple obedience in their eyes—well, obedience *most* of the time!" he chuckled, remembering the ram that had constantly tested his patience when he was a lad.

"The two-legged variety I shepherd now are much less loyal than the four-legged kind, and much more like mules than sheep." David had grown serious while reflecting.

"Father, please! Sing for us," begged Solomon again, quickly bringing him back to the present. "Forget the people for a moment."

"All right, son," the king conceded, the concern visibly leaving his face. "But remember, you will be the shepherd soon and must know their ways well enough to love them anyway and lead them wisely without becoming discouraged."

"Just sing, my lord," Bathsheba sweetly coaxed him. "Solomon will be a good and wise king, don't you worry."

So David sang to his son the words he loved to hear.

Blessed is the man who fears the Lord,
Who finds great delight in His commands.
His children are mighty in the land;
The generation of the upright will be blessed.

Wealth and riches are in his house,
And his righteousness endures forever!

Even in darkness, light dawns for the upright,
For the gracious and compassionate and righteous man.
Good comes to him who is generous and kind,
Who conducts his affairs with justice.
The Lord hears the cry of the broken hearted,
And his righteousness endures forever![1]

As the chords died away, Solomon asked quickly, "Father, tell me again: What makes a man righteous?"

David picked out a mystical melody on the strings for background. Then, carefully choosing phrases from several of his songs, he spoke rather than sang the answer to his son.

A righteous man
Trusts in the Lord with all his heart
And leans not unto his own understanding.[2]
He judges impartially, he hates evil,
But he loves mercy and truth.
He fears no evil because God's hand protects him
And is upon his life forever.

A righteous man
Weeps over his sin and blames no one else,
And then repents deeply, crying out to his God.
He forgives as he has been forgiven.
He thinks of himself as grass that withers and fades
And will one day be seen no more.
He rests in the love of God alone.

---

1   Adapted from Psalm 112:1b-6.
2   Adapted from Proverbs 3:5.

A righteous man
Cares not for the praise of mere men
But hungers for the praise of his God.
He delights in the Lord and loves His laws
And commits all his ways to Him.
If he stumbles, he will not fall
For the Lord will uphold him with his right hand.

A righteous man
Knows that his life is precious to God,
That it was God who knit him in his mother's womb,
And his days are ordained by the Lord.
His riches are given by his loving God,
And he will never need to beg bread.
His trust in God will bring him blessing forever.[3]

The king's voice ceased and his fingers lay still upon the strings. A hush fell over the room—the very air pregnant with the presence of God. And David began to prophesy:

The Lord reigns,
Let the nations tremble;
He sits enthroned between the cherubim,
Let the earth shake!
Great is the Lord in Zion;
He is exalted over all the nations!

Let them praise Your great and awesome name—
He is holy!

The King is mighty, he loves justice—
You have established equity;

⌒ ──────── ⌒

3   Taken from Psalm 1:2; 119:113; 37:24; 63:8; 139:13,16; 37:25.

In Jacob you have done
What is just and right.
Exalt the Lord our God
And worship at His footstool;

For He is holy![4]

The Promise Revealed

After a long silence David spoke solemnly to his son. "Solomon," the king began, "you will be king for a season, and God will love and discipline you as a son. He will never take His presence from you and through you will be established God's reign in Israel forever!" His voice rose in intensity. "This God has promised." Tears filled the king's eyes and then spilled down his cheeks.

"But there is One to come, One who will sit at the right hand of God and rule the earth in *perfect* righteousness for endless ages. You and I are just His forebearers, shadows of the One who will come." He openly wept for several minutes. Bathsheba and her son, tears in their eyes as well, waited for the king to recover.

When all was quiet again, David laid his lyre aside and leaned toward Solomon, their eyes fixed upon each other. "I tell you the truth," David said with conviction, "there is a King of Israel coming someday who will not only break the power of human bondage, but of sin as well!"

Then, forgetting everyone else in the room, David whispered to himself, "How I long to see the day He rides into Jerusalem!"

Solomon, however captivated by such a thought, could only wonder at his father's dream.

4   Psalm 99:1-5.

Of Things to Come

The king's face darkened and he spoke again to his son. "However, God has shown me that before He reigns, we will kill Him! He will be pierced and mocked and despised by His own people! Our shame will be upon Him as He dies!" At this, Solomon started in his seat.

Before his son could protest, David asserted, "But somehow He will live again!" Then shaking his head, he said, "Don't ask me to explain that, but I know it is true! He *will* reign from Zion over all the earth!"

He hadn't meant to reveal all this to his son without warning. He hadn't discussed it with anyone since he and his own father Jesse had shared secrets that day in Bethlehem many years ago. But he was relieved to release it at last to the one who most needed to know.

Of course, it was woven into many of the songs that were sung before the Ark of the Covenant, but he knew the people comprehended little of what they were singing, which always made his heart ache. Someday they would understand. Someday.

Returning to them again, David rose from his couch, stretched and flashed a warm smile at Solomon.

"That's enough for tonight! Meet me at the palace entrance early in the morning, right after prayer," the king instructed his son. "I have some plans to show you, young man. I think it's time for action!"

Puzzled but excited, Solomon retired that night with many mysteries scurrying about in his head and heart. What he was able to grasp, he held onto tightly. He could see that he would need great wisdom—much more than he already had—in order to fulfill the mandate upon his life.

Chapter Twenty-seven

THE FINAL VICTORY

Before the sun began its gentle assault on the nighttime darkness, David was awake and up. After donning his robe to fend off the chill, he quickly lit the lamp on his nightstand and carried it to the other side of the room. As the lamp cast a soft circle of light over his ornately hand-carved cedar desk, he reached into a secret compartment and pulled out several scrolls upon which his scribe had written some 30 years before. On the yellowed parchment were the plans for the temple that God had promised David his son would build.

After making sure they were all there, he put them into a leather pouch that he would carry to the building site in a few hours. Then he picked up the chair belonging to his desk and placed it near his eastern window. After unlatching and opening the shutters, he adjusted it to face the night sky and sat down.

Next, he drew his beloved lyre onto his lap and began to sing his praises to God as he did every morning before prayer. Although his fingers were a bit stiff with age, the music was as sweet as when he had played for King Saul so long ago.

My heart is steadfast, O God!
I will sing and make music with all my soul!
Awake, harp and lyre!
I will awaken the dawn.

As he sang to the Lord, the sky began to lighten.

I will praise You, O Lord, among the nations;
I will sing of You among the peoples,
For great is Your love
And faithfulness to me.

Be exalted, O God, above the heavens,
Let Your glory be over all the earth![1]

The sun's rays pierced the clouds that hung upon the horizon, casting a soft pink hue upon the city and the hills beyond.

David put aside the lyre and began his prayers.

On the Mountain

At the appointed time, David and Solomon met and walked the distance to the highest point on Mt. Moriah, talking excitedly all the way. By the time they had arrived, the sun was high in the sky and David had shared with his son his dreams and the story of how God had given to him the plans he had tucked inside the pouch slung over his shoulder.

Once there, they paced off the property and determined the future lay of the entire temple, according to the specifications recorded on the scrolls. Amazingly, the altar for the temple was to go exactly where David had been told to make a sacrifice to end the plague a few years before!

"Do you realize what this means?" asked Solomon, his hand on his father's arm. "Even though you must die before the temple is built, you have participated in offerings to the Lord right here already!" he said with wonder in his voice. "How loving of God to use even your repentance for sin to bless you and give you a part in your own vision!"

━━━━━━━━━

1   Adapted from Psalm 57:7-11.

David, who wept so easily, wept again with sobs that shook his now frail frame.

He lifted his eyes to Heaven. "How can I repay You for all Your goodness to me?" he implored the heavens, his voice choked with tears.

Images and Shadows

The day was passing quickly, and as they stood in awe before the simple altar, the plaintive cries of sheep broke the hush that had descended upon the Mount. It was 3:00 in the afternoon—the hour designated by Moses for sacrificing the Passover lamb! As David looked at the altar, with the bleating of sheep in his ears, he saw in his heart the Lamb lying there who had died for him so long ago…and fresh tears blinded him.

He's coming! The King is Coming! It will be soon! David said to himself, his heart pounding at the thought.

Turning to Solomon, for whom this whole scene remained shrouded in mystery, the king said with resolve, "We must prepare for the building immediately. All materials can be ready before I die!"

Then refocusing upon the altar, David said as though to the Lamb, "I don't need to be here, do I? I have seen the temple in my heart and have worshiped You in the Holy of Holies deep within my spirit. For me, it is finished."

As he dried his eyes on the edge of his royal robe, David smiled and remarked wonderingly to the heavens, "Perhaps even this temple will be but a shadow…"

Going Home

At sunset, emotionally exhausted but exhilarated, the king leaned upon the arm of the king-to-be as they walked the dusty road back to Jerusalem. To his left in the distance, now in the evening shadow of Mt. Moriah, was the Mount of Olives where he had wept and prayed before crossing Jordan, when it seemed that his nation had rejected him as king.

Glancing to his right, he saw the hill on which the sheep had been bleating at the hour of sacrifice. David started suddenly and very nearly lost his footing as the shadows—playing games in the fading light—formed not one, but *three* crossed beams against the distant hills beyond!

"Are you all right, Father?" Solomon asked, concerned when David almost fell when accosted by the illusive sight.

"Yes, son. I am fine," he answered a bit unsteadily.

They continued on in silence.

And then, ahead of him, again for only his eyes to see, walked a simply-clad shepherd cradling a wounded lamb in his arms!

The Lord is my shepherd, I shall not want... echoed from childhood in the spirit of the aging king as he followed close behind.

As they neared the city walls, David stopped to rest. For some reason, he turned to look back through the twilight at Mt. Moriah, and what he saw took his breath away! It was as if he were 12 years old again, standing with his brothers on a hill outside Bethlehem!

Eyes in the Night Sky

The final stage of the vision that had split the evening sky above the family altar was now, in the space of an instant, being played out in the heavens directly above the future site of the Temple!

The sky was filled with angels weeping as they waited at the crossed beams, while winged dragons—talons bared and breathing fire—towered over them in victory.

It was exactly as it had been all those long years ago...

And then the glistening contour of a throne—the great size of which had never been seen on earth—emerged in the heavens where the beams had but a moment before stood.

As David strained to see the mysterious King upon the mystical golden throne, sudden bursts of brilliant color blinded him for a moment! His hands flew to his face to cover his smarting eyes.

But with his eyes closed, as though etched upon the inside of his eyelids, the face of the Lamb appeared as well, seated on the throne beside the King! Both wore crowns upon their heads.

And the eyes of the King and the Lamb were the same...

As David slowly opened his own eyes again, only dragons and angels remained. The combat was on! But before a single talon could strike a blow, the dragons were slain as the angels' swords flashed with lightning speed!

As the dragons gasped in death, the angels danced above them and sang in triumph,

> *To Him who sits on the throne*
> *And to the Lamb,*
> *Be praise and honor and glory and power,*
> *For ever and ever! Amen!*[2]

Again, Solomon asked with concern, "Are you all right, Father?"

"Yes, son," he smiled. "I'm ready to go Home now."

2   Revelation 5:13b.

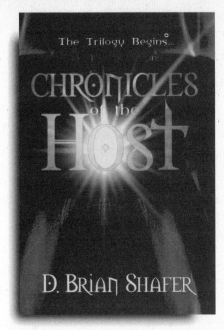

The Trilogy Begins...

CHRONICLES
of the
HOST

D. BRIAN SHAFER

Coming Soon

CHRONICLES OF THE HOST
By D. Brian Shafer

Gabriel lived just a short distance from Lucifer. The residences were situated on the same street—but what a difference! Whereas Lucifer indulged himself with great splendor, living in the largest house in Heaven (apart from the heavenly Temple), Gabriel chose to live quite modestly. Lucifer felt it unbecoming of so highly regarded an angel as Gabriel to live in such a plain manner, but it was very much like Gabriel to live this way, as he was one of the most unassuming and humble angels in all of Heaven.

Gabriel was everyone's friend and confidant. He was well loved and respected, quick of mind, playful almost to the point of rowdiness. But the most endearing quality about him was that one could entrust himself to Gabriel. This is not to say that the other angels were not trustworthy, but only that Gabriel's very person invited one's trust without reservation, a special gift from the Lord. It was to nobody's surprise therefore, when the Lord announced that Gabriel was to become the Messenger of the Kingdom, for who better to serve as messenger than the one angel everyone called a friend, and in whom everyone trusted?

"Michael! Over here!" called a voice from the garden in front of the house.

Michael turned to see Gabriel standing under a magnificent tree, motioning Michael over and eating a piece of fruit.

"Hello, Gabriel," answered Michael. "Or is it Lord Gabriel now?" he added, borrowing from Lucifer's greeting to him earlier.

"Lord Gabriel," said Gabriel, embracing Michael. "I've got to admit it sounds strange putting those two words together, doesn't it?"

"Yes, like lord and Lucifer," Michael answered. "Now there is a disturbing combination, to say the least."

Gabriel immediately drew the conclusion. "I suppose you've been to see our friend?"

Michael nodded. "Here, let's sit down," Gabriel said, tossing Michael a large yellowish green piece of fruit and motioning for them to settle themselves under the lush branches of the tree.

As they sat down, their attention was suddenly drawn to a fast moving figure walking in front of the house. It was Serus, carrying the newly created music for Gabriel's service. He saw the two angels seated under the tree, gave a quick nod of acknowledgment to them, and went on his way. They watched him disappear down the street.

"That poor angel," said Michael, remembering Serus' curt dismissal by Lucifer earlier. He shook his head.

"Who, Serus?" remarked Gabriel. "I should be so poor, living in the finest place in Heaven." He looked for a reaction from Michael and went on. "I know a few angels who would like to have his position. I mean, serving Lucifer is quite an honor." Michael remained impassive. Gabriel casually bit into the fruit and continued, "Of course, I suppose there is a price to pay for serving someone as temperamental as…"

"Temperamental!" Michael finally exploded to Gabriel's amusement. "Lucifer is more than temperamental. What I saw today was simply unreasonable."

Gabriel's interest was awakened as Michael recounted the events of the meeting with Lucifer, the mocking of Serus as a potential archangel followed by his curt dismissal, the uneasy atmosphere when they were discussing Gabriel's promotion, and the uncomfortable feeling that accompanied him as he left the house. Gabriel listened intently to Michael's story. Then an amused look came over his face, as if he were imagining a scene far away in his mind.

"Wouldn't it be something if Serus ever *was* made an archangel?" he said. "I would not want to be around Lucifer on that day!"

"Is that all you can say?" said an exasperated Michael. "You've missed the whole point." He stood up, facing the Mountain in the North, squinting at its brillance.

"All right, Michael," said Gabriel, looking at his good friend. "What exactly are you trying to tell me? That Lucifer is bizarre and difficult to be around sometimes?" Michael turned around to look at Gabriel. "Everyone in Heaven knows that. If Serus ever wants to leave Lucifer's service he can do so anytime. He doesn't have to stay. He chooses to stay."

Michael's face softened. "I don't know, my brother," he said. "Except that he is so unlike the way he once was. We were all such good friends. Now I hardly ever see him unless it is in offical service to the Most High." He looked at Gabriel, his eyes teary, and went on. "I miss the old Lucifer…our friend Lucifer…the Lucifer who roamed the Kingdom with us from one end to the other…the Lucifer who laughed harder than any of us…the Lucifer who brought us joy and set our hearts to dancing…our brother the Morning Star."

Gabriel put his hand on Michael's shoulder. "I miss him too, Michael." He looked into Michael's eyes, filled with compassion. "Perhaps you're right. Maybe we can talk to him together and find out if something is wrong."

As he finished saying this Gabriel spotted Serus on his way back to Lucifer's house. Once again the little angel nodded a quick greeting and scurried off. "But one thing is certain," said Gabriel as they both watched Serus move down the street. "There is definitely a price to pay for serving Lucifer!" They both laughed and headed into Gabriel's house.

<u>Coming in 2003</u>
The Chronicles continue with…
Book Two—*Bloody Swath*
Book Three—*Final Confrontation*

Available at your local Christian bookstore.